The Last Judgment

THE LAST JUDGMENT

Jonathan Lee

BOLD PUBLISHING

Library of Congress Control Number: 2023911254

Cover photograph by jplenio via Pixabay

ISBN: 979-8-9884392-1-9

Bold Publishing is a small independent publishing imprint.
Your support is greatly appreciated.

For Mom

I

SHE had never known her mother, and now she was burying her father. A shallow grave dug with a rusted shovel. A mound of mud and snow to one side in the pale mountain twilight. The fading sunlight skimmed along the peak edge to the south, stretching out long shadows of the surrounding conifers.

She paused for a moment. The cold slushy dirt covered all but his face now. A pale face that contrasted sharply with the dark bushy beard that covered it. A serene expressionless expression lay over that tranquil face, free of the pain that had plagued him in his final days. No more wincing, tears, or choking gasps. He was resting in peace.

With a simple nod and a long blink, she covered his calm countenance last and continued piling the rest of the soil over his grave. By the time she was finished, the sun had set beyond the distant peaks. In the dimmest of remaining light of the early evening, she trudged back across the snow-laden forest floor, further up the slope to the old cabin.

She gave a final glance back down the gentle slope, but all she could see now was darkness. And so, with a sigh, she turned around and closed the door. She curled up to the wood fire, and covered herself in a blanket. There she began to sob. Her father had wanted her to be strong. Even being dead, she couldn't shed a tear in his presence. And besides, outside it was too cold to cry.

◊

She carried on for several days, carrying out the quiet labor needed for her survival. Gathering deadwood for kindling. Chopping logs. Tending to the food forest. At one point, she fondled some pine needles in her hand, deciding whether to make tea. She had delicately caressed her belly, and gazed toward it, before letting go of the little green bundle in her hand. She had another bundle to be concerned about now. Her sack. She would need room in it for more essential items on her journey.

She had lived on Sky Island her whole life. 17 years and a season or two, according to her father. The only other person she had ever known. Together they lived in a little log cabin in a valley with a view to the peak of Old Man Mountain in the west. Occasionally she would hike that direction with her father at certain times of the year when the waterfall was flowing down Old Man's face. At other times, they would head east and take the southward trail up to the top of Old Man's head. From there, standing upon his bald gravel-capped head, they could see for many miles around Sky Island and beyond. The first time her father let her look through his spyglass, it was like magic.

A phase of the moon had passed before she finally made up her mind. Her deer skin satchel was full of supplies. Little leather pouches of berries and pine nuts and almonds. The last of which were particularly precious, being from the almond tree growing alone in the food forest. She also had a bit of birch bark and cedar wood, for tinder and firewood respectively. She had fitted the satchel in the center of her backpack frame—a triangular form, made of wood, with leather straps attached—and alongside it a bedroll, a tent bundle, a quiver of arrows, a canteen, and a hunting knife. She had thought about taking the little mirror hanging up in the cabin with her, but it seemed like too much of an indulgence.

On the last night of her preparations, the moon was out in full, slowly gliding between a lane of coniferous canopy. She gazed up at Mother Moon and whispered a little prayer. "Silver lady, please guide my steps through the dark and send me dreams of wisdom in my sleep."

She turned her eyes back to the fire, and let out a sigh. She waited for a moment of quiet reflection, as firelight danced in her eyes. The only sounds were the crackles, sizzles, and pops of the little fiery heap, the hissing roast of the bird carcass suspended above it, and the chirping song of crickets in the distant dark. The aroma of smoke and charred gamey flesh wafted through the air. When the moment passed, she gave a final nod to herself and let out another sigh, before removing her dinner, putting out the fire, and heading back to the cabin. Tonight would be her last night sleeping within its walls.

◇

The next morning, she awoke at dawn, got dressed, gathered up her pack, and stepped out into the cold crystal air of a mid-autumn day in the forest. She was greeted with the music of songbirds. Music which was cut short when she took several crunchy steps out on the snow. The scent of pine danced on the air as the forest canopy swayed in the breeze above her, bringing to her ears that oceanic sound of wind blowing through pine needles.

She trudged down the slope to her father's grave, and there, stopped. She lowered herself to her knees, clasped her hands together, closed her eyes, and started to whisper.

"I'm… doing what you asked, father." A moment of silence. Birdsong returned from the distance in the now still air. She clenched her eyes. Tried to hold them tight to fight away the tears. Gulped them down and continued.

"I-I need your help. Father. I need you. Please be with me. I can't do this alone. Please be with me. Please be—please be by my side." She bit her lips now, and clenched her eyes as tight as she could. "Papa, please…"

Cold tears rolled down her cheeks. She wiped them away, quickly. Sniffed them away. Rose to her feet in anger. Anger at herself. Anger at her loss of control, perceived weakness and folly. Burning quietly inside was another anger. An anger she wouldn't admit. Couldn't admit.

With one last sniff, she turned and marched on. And she never looked back.

II

S HE hiked for six straight hours, taking the trail up to the south ridge line, before continuing along the ridge east for several miles. She had climbed over 3,000 feet, passing from lush forest up through rugged cliffs to the bare rocky ridge line. In that time, she had traversed nearly 12 miles over rugged terrain, before she stopped for a midday meal. A ration of fowl meat, a handful of berries, and a few sips from her canteen.

Once she plopped down and caught her breath, the soft rushing babble of distant streams came to her ears, in between the whooshing blow of an occasional autumn breeze. From up on the ridge, she could, at times, see past the rolling hills all around to the vast desert beyond. Her father had told her it was the reason the land was called Sky Island.

"In other parts of the world, islands are surrounded by many waters," her father had told her one day on a hike.

"Waters?" she had asked.

"Yes, large pools of water. So large, they stretch out as far as you can see. Even with a spyglass. The water goes out beyond the horizon."

She replied quietly with a cock of her head and an incredulous smirk. She couldn't tell if he was teasing her, as he sometimes did.

"I'm serious," he said with a chuckle. "They called it the *ocean*."

"Ocean?"

He replied with a nod, before continuing. "Of course, that's far from here. Here, our island is surrounded by nothing more, nor less, than sand and sky."

Back in the present, those last words lingered in her mind. *Sand and sky*. There had to be more. What secrets were hiding amidst those ruins? Maybe only death. But if death lay before her, it certainly lay behind. She might as well move forward into an uncertain future than stay behind in the certainty of solitude.

◇

As she descended from the ridge line down into the south valley, the landscape steadily changed. The conifers, which were so plentiful on the north side of the ridge, quickly faded away. Small patches of melting snow lay between short shrubs which dotted the southern slopes, along with a sparse smattering of leafless trees. Skeletal trees which lingered in the land like the gnarled fractal remnants of an age long passed.

She stopped for a moment to catch her breath to take one last look at the view beyond, out into the distant ruins. With her spyglass, she could barely make them out. Crumbling structures out in the haze beyond the mountains. At the end, one stood out—and always had for years. The great pyramid. Like a little mountain of its own, but with straight lines and perfect angles, and it wasn't much taller than the other structures—at least as far as she could see.

Marching lower and lower, the air slowly grew warmer. She followed the trail of a sandy wash, snaking its way down the sloping terrain, flanked by an assortment of bushes growing in the rocky soil. Towards the middle of the afternoon, the terrain grew greener, but the air was no cooler as she descended deeper into the valley. She refilled her canteen in a nearby stream, and picked a few wild herbs and berries, before continuing along the wash. Ahead, she knew she would soon approach the final boundary of her world: The dead lakes.

◇

As the sun set in the west—having already descended beyond the western hills of the valley in which she hiked—she could make out the long shadows of unusually tall trees, looming in the south. They marked the northern edge of the larger of the two dead lakes. Empty clay-lined pools, surrounded by a graveyard of trees. Decaying, leafless poplars and redwoods. Fruitless fruit trees. Ominous skeletal forms reaching up to a darkening sky in the early twilight of a long day, now passing away.

She passed by those dead trees and crossed a rickety old bridge. A worn wood bridge which spanned the empty channel connecting two dead lakes. On the other side of that bridge was a road. Torn up asphalt, barely recognizable between all the cracks and holes filled with grass and scrub. She took a parting gaze behind her at the snow capped mountain to the north, before turning back and stepping out onto that old, chewed up road. It was the farthest point away she had ever been.

The road turned left to the east, and she followed it a couple dozen yards to the lodge. A simple single story structure, crumbling under years of neglect, surrounded by dead poplars and a line of wood railing. The railing was white once. The last vestiges of crinkling paint barely visible in the failing light.

It was as good of a stop as any. She could use the shelter for the night. But there was no time to waste now, using what little light there was left to collect kindling and firewood. She used the water in her canteen to make soup with the last of her rations. When she was finally ready to sleep for the night, she carefully tread inside, carrying a single flaming twig to guide her way. With the tiny torch in one hand, she gestured a little warding sign over herself, tapping each shoulder and her forehead to make the sacred triangle, before crawling her way through the building to an old bed.

III

SHE awoke the following morning with the soft light of an unseen sun streaming through the window of the eastern room where she slept. Shards of glass twinkled in the early light. The remnants of the window's broken pane.

She slowly lifted herself from that dusty, dilapidated mattress. She stretched and yawned, rubbed the sleep out of her eyes, and took a deep breath before crossing the debris-laden floor and walking out into the chill morning air. Not nearly as cold as yesterday. But she was prepared for warmer days ahead. How much warmer, she wasn't sure.

A little ways in the west, lit by the golden light of the sun just now reaching over the hills in the east, stood a solitary fruit tree. An apple tree. The lone miraculous survivor of devastating neglect. She harvested as many apples as she could reasonably carry, before carrying on.

The cracked, crumbling road continued south from the lodge for over three miles before another road met it. A road which wasn't much more than a wide dirt trail, running perpendicular to the road she was on. It crossed the wash she had been following and ran up into the hills of the valley, backtracking north and then snaking back south and then turning again. Beyond that, she couldn't see, but it likely bore east.

She took a sip from her canteen and thought for a moment, before taking this new road. And thus her slow climb began through a narrower valley, meandering its way through the mountains east on a road that crisscrossed with a nearby wash. After hiking for more than an hour through this new wilderness, a gradual bend gave way to a steady decline. She walked on for another couple hours, getting lower and lower through winding courses and switchbacks. The mountains became more dramatic over this time. Layers of sediment painting subtle bands of color over the rock face.

After one final bend to the east, she emerged out between strange rocky bluffs, the likes of which she had never seen before. And beyond that canyon, she could see low-lying hills reaching up out of flat dusty land. She continued on this path for another quarter hour, before coming to another artifact of older times. A metal sign with some of the word markings she had seen before in certain parts of Sky Island. The dirt road she was on flared out into a circle, flanked on one side by rotting wood railings. But strangest of all was something out along the trail beyond the circle.

It was like a metal tent, but with wheels. She picked up her pace to meet it. Any caution sacrificed for the sake of curiosity. It was red with rust. Any paint that had once been on it had long since peeled away. It was surrounded by a smattering of broken glass. Inside was some kind of seating behind a little wheel about the size of her forearm.

"Car?" she heard herself blurt out. Her father had told her of such a thing, but she had never seen it with her own eyes.

Away from the trail, and beyond the wash, something else caught her attention. It wasn't far from the old rusted metal machine, almost as though the car was pointing at it. Some kind of writing perhaps, but different from the ones on the signs. She jogged for a couple minutes to the rock wall, jaunting along like an excited child at play. It was some kind of drawings, etched in the rock. One looked like some manner of insect. Another vaguely similar to a stick figure of a man. Haphazard, seemingly symbolic figures carved in the rock at some point of an indeterminate past.

"Huh," she snorted to herself with a furrowed brow and a slack jaw. Between the strange petroglyphs and the rusted car, what other wonders might there be in the world?

IV

SHE traveled for less than a mile, before she came to another fork in the road. In that time, she had passed by some shambling ruins similar to the ones she knew back on Sky Island. Brown signs with indecipherable text next to stone tables. A crumbling wooden shack with that symbol of the strange man sitting on his circular chair. The similarity of these things to what she knew back up on the mountain top was curious, but not enough for her to stop.

At the fork, she decided to turn left and up, but after a matter of minutes she came across a series of metal signs that made her change her mind. They were similar to the yellow one she saw before, but when she passed by she could faintly make out gray pictograph outlines, like shadows against the dim yellow of the rusted metal diamonds. There were two to either side of the road, both depicting a figure of a man, walking. Above one was a third that showed what looked like a man perched above some four-legged creature. Below each set were rectangular placards with faint arrows, both apparently pointing at the road. When she looked off to the south at her left, there was a thin dirt path trailing away, amidst the creosote and assorted scrub dotting the rocky soil.

Could this be the way to people? She must be getting closer.

◇

She wandered for over an hour through the arid wilderness, along that dirt trail in the growing heat of an increasingly late morning. When the sun was nearly overhead, she came across another outcropping of artifice. An array of dark panels of some kind in front of a series of tan brick structures, all in front of a crumbling asphalt road. A whole little network of roads, in fact.

She veered off the trail and headed straight toward the structures, careful to avoid the yucca palms and cacti that speckled the landscape, along with desert broom and other flora.

"Hello?" she called out in a bit of naive hope.

The only answer she received was the sudden flutter of wings, as a flock of grackles scattered into the air at the sound of her voice. The flapping commotion of the birds reminded her that she would need to hunt again.

"Don't focus on the arrow," her father had said in a whisper. "Keep your eye on your target. Right at the center of her body. Watch her closely. Don't just see where she's been, but where she's going. Anticipate. Predict. Even breaths. In and out. When you're ready… let it go."

He had been standing beside her on the slope, between the trees, guiding her hands and speaking in her ear in a hushed tone. When she let the arrow fly, it struck the deer right in the heart. She snapped her face to her father and gasped.

"I did it!" she exclaimed, albeit quietly. A smile started to creep across the corners of her mouth, below bright beaming young eyes. A smile that was met by her father with a warm, but mostly blank, expression. He slowly blinked and nodded his head. She turned her own back toward the deer. A young doe who was struggling to scurry away. Fumbling and flailing as it darted off in pain, its life quickly bleeding out.

Her smile had quickly faded into quiet horror, as she beheld the sight. Her first kill. A final moment of innocence that was fading away, with every beat of the doe's heart. A young doe, not much more than a year old. Likely she had never had a fawn of her own. And now here she lay, far from whatever herd she may have had, her life abruptly ended in the midst of fear and confusion.

"Thank you, sister, for the gift of your flesh," her father intoned somberly as they knelt near the lifeless creature. The little ritual brought some measure of peace. Some measure of meaning and justification for the violence. And for the years that followed, it was enough. But in that moment, it felt a bit like binding a broken staff with cedar rope. The staff would hold together for a time, but it was no longer whole.

Now, back in the desert, something at the periphery of her sight caught her eye. A scurrying of a little mammal out in the bushes. She recognized its form immediately. The species she had encountered in the mountains was a little different, but very similar. A cottontail rabbit. Several, in fact, bounding in the distance.

She pulled an arrow from her quiver and tested it against her bow string, solemnly. Tonight she would eat well enough. She glanced toward the bright, burning sun above. Next, she would need to somehow find more water…

Jonathan Lee

V

AFTER an hour along the road, she came to a fork and took the smaller road to her right to veer south. After another hour on the meandering course, she came to a concrete drainage way. The drainage way was bordered by a rocky mound to the north and a row of abandoned houses to the east. The mound rose from the desert floor about 50 feet or so. She could climb it to get a better view of the city. Those ruins she saw from afar so long ago up on Sky Island.

In the meantime, she spotted something at the bottom of that concrete canal. Water. Several small puddles had collected at the bottom of the ramp-like incline. She had been walking slowly. Pacing herself in the heat of the day, as her father had told her to do—were she to ever actually walk in the desert. But now she picked up the pace before eventually bursting into a run toward a muddy pool.

When she got to it, she emptied out the rest of her canteen into herself. Swallowing down those last few precious sips she had been saving. She then gathered up the bit of water there, scraping the canteen along the ground to get every bit she could, and racing from puddle to puddle. The last remnants of an autumn rain that fell two nights ago.

Her canteen was full. Later, when the sun set, she would boil the water. But now it was time to get a lay of the land.

And so she climbed that gray tan hill nearby to its modest summit, and looked out on the ruins. The quiet crumbling remains of a vast metropolis, stretching out in every direction to distant mountain ranges along the white-blue haze at the horizon.

With her spyglass, she spotted it again. She could nearly see it with her naked eye at this point. The great pyramid. Looming near distant structures at the other edge of the city. It was farther off than she imagined, but closer than she had ever seen it before.

◇

She stopped for a small midday snack in the backyard of one of the ruins. A two-story tan stucco estate with dusty windows nearly the same color as the walls. There in the shade, she chewed through a couple of apples in quiet contemplation. A cool breeze blew from the east, as birds faintly chattered and cawed in the distance. The wind carried the faint odor of sand and creosote. As she surveyed the surroundings, it wasn't what she was used to, but it had its own peculiar charm. She could get used to it. Assuming she could survive in it…

Once she decided to get moving again, she followed a little road on the other side of the estate wall. Over the course of an hour, this road snaked along rows of abandoned homes. Once lavish suburban estates, now surrounded by skeletal trees and dusty, cracked patios. After that hour, this stream-like road on the edge of the city finally flowed its way through to the interior.

As she followed that last bend past the first cross street, she faced a sight which filled her face with an open smile. The pyramid. She could see the tip of it, glinting in the sunlight, off in the distance. It was still a ways yet, but she could behold it with naked eyes now. She picked up her pace at the sight, and kept steadily marching that way for much of the rest of her journey.

◇

Nearly three hours had passed. Marching past rows of palm trees and stucco homes. Rows of skeletal trees and crumbling buildings. The road had grown wide. At least 70 feet across. Like a dark river of black rock. A wide lane of asphalt with more cracks in it than a lizard's skin. Occasionally, between some of those cracks would rise up grass. Some green, some brown.

At one point, another great river of a road passed over the one she was on. A kind of great bridge, crossing overhead, suspended by vast columns of concrete. Several times she passed by rusted vehicles along the road, or in alcoves of asphalt to one side or another. The sight started to become so ubiquitous, in fact, it lost all novelty. In all of it, she never stopped, as she was determined to reach the pyramid by nightfall.

She didn't know what she would find there. Heading all this way east had been something of a detour, in fact. At least if what her father had told her was true. But before she took *that* journey, she had to see the pyramid—at least once in her life. She had spent so many years wondering.

And so after a couple turns on to other streets and progressively making her way east and ever so slightly south, she came to it at last. The great pyramid. Its western face was lit up with dazzling brightness as the sun reflected off its otherwise obsidian surface. She jogged along the road for several hundred feet, as she looked up at the strange structure in excited awe.

As she came around to its backside, however, she saw something she hadn't anticipated. A giant statue of sorts at the base of the pyramid. It was itself several stories tall. Only a fraction of the size of the pyramid, but looming large nevertheless. Several tunnels cut through its bottom. She passed under it, and through it, coming out a walkway to the east to behold a massive face of a man perched above the body of a creature like a wild cat of some sort. Beneath the man's massive chin was a statue of another smaller man perched atop the arch under which she passed. Past the end of the walkway, on the other side of some elevated railings, was a stone obelisk.

Some word markings were etched onto the obelisk's face. In fact, all throughout the campus she was now touring, there were markings here and there. Some seemingly similar to the ones she saw back on Sky Island, and others very different indeed.

At the foot of the massive statue's literal feet, there at the end of the walkway, was a series of doors leading into some enclosed interior. She cautiously made her way inside, to find she was inside a tube-like house of many windows. The window and wall to the south was strangely sloping, and outside she could see beyond to the metal rails she saw before, extending off into the distance.

It would appear she was now standing in some kind of "car," perhaps, but quite different from any she had seen before. It was a comparatively large space with benches and periodic metal poles. She had passed by a concrete bench down in the tunnel before, but these seats seemed more comfortable. It might be a nice place to sleep for the night.

And so, as the sun set on the other side of the great pyramid, beyond the distant mountains of her old home, she lit a fire under the tunnel. She had found a concrete container of some kind along the road, and it seemed to make a decent fire pit of sorts. She could easily roast her game, after she had finished skinning it.

After her meal of roasted rabbit stew and apples, she decided to sleep in the strange car. She curled up on a bench inside and fell asleep, mostly sated. Tomorrow would be less certain. Water being her biggest concern. If she couldn't find what she needed here in the city, she wondered what hope there was of finding it out beyond the Valley of Death. But she knew she needed to take this journey one step at a time. And so she cleared her mind and quieted her heart. Tomorrow's cares could wait until then.

Jonathan Lee

28

VI

"PAPA?" she heard herself asking in the midst of a groggy fog. She awoke in confusion, unsure where she was or why. She had thought she heard her father's voice, but remembered with some pain that he was gone. And she was gone too. Here so far away from her mountain home. Nevertheless, she could have sworn she heard a voice like her father's. The cruel trick of a sleepy mind, no doubt. But then it came again…

"I said it may not be advisable to sleep in the tram."

She bolted up in her seat at the sound of the voice. Instinctively, she grabbed for her hunting knife. Her heart raced, and her lungs pumped excited quivering breaths through her drool-filled mouth. Sleep painfully left every part of her body as she scrambled into action, pointing the knife out defensively.

"I mean you no harm," he said in the same even-tempered voice. And she could see him raising his arms up in a conciliatory gesture, as he slowly backed away from one of the doors. The broken half open door, on a diagonal within its frame. Through that triangular opening, she could see more of his form, as he stepped out into the morning light, beyond the shadow in which he had been.

"Gah!" she exclaimed. A shouting gasp of shock and confused horror. The man was some kind of strange, nearly skeletal form. Glowing blue eyes, beneath a smooth bald head, on a strange anthropic face of… metal? Painted white perhaps, but peeling in places, like many things in the world.

He looked back at her and slowly blinked. A strangely serene expression on his quiet face. Aside from the blink, he remained motionless. Still as a statue. So much so that for a moment, she thought perhaps she had gone mad.

She shook the thought away and shouted in a trembling voice, "Wha-what are you?"

He cocked his head for a moment in silence, and darted his eyes back and forth as though thinking. Then, after a brief moment, he replied, "That is not exactly a simple question to answer. I suppose I am… what I am. What that is precisely would be difficult to articulate, and I would need to understand you better to do so, in a manner that is effectively communicative."

"What? I… are you—are you some kind of demon?" she asked with a gulp.

"Demon? Hm," he replied, again cocking his head in seeming contemplation. "No, I do not believe that would adequately describe my modality of being. I suppose it would depend upon your ontological perspective. To be frank, I am not certain such entities truly exist. Whatever I may be, I am certain I *am*. Accordingly, 'demon' would not appear to be an appropriate appellation."

"I—I don't understand," she said in between pants, the knife still trembling in her hands.

"I apologize. It has proven to be a persistent challenge adjusting my idiolect in order to effectively communicate with… humans."

"So… you're not human?" she asked with a frown.

"I am afraid not."

"You're afraid?"

"Afraid *not*. It is a colloquial expression, I suppose. I am not truly experiencing fear. At least not to any notable extent."

She tried to catch her breath. Tried to slow it down. And after a moment, she slowly arose, still holding the knife out in front of her. The metal man took a step back as she did.

"You may not be afraid," she said, "and I may be... but I'm not afraid to use *this*."

"I am afraid it would do little good. That is to say, it would be ineffective. If it *were* effective, it would still do little good, as the potential for damage would be very bad to be sure. Fortunately, for me, the exterior shell, housing my vital components, is mostly composed of a titanium alloy that your knife would be unable to penetrate. Accordingly—"

"Are you taunting me?"

"No, I bear no ill will toward you."

"But you-you're saying that I... I can't hurt you?"

He paused and cocked his head a moment. A quick little gesture, almost like a bird. "You would not be able to damage me physically. If my assessment is correct, your body composition is incapable of kinetically generating the necessary amount of joules to overcome the tensile strength of my body's exterior with your weapon."

He seemed to be answering her question in the affirmative, as far as she could tell, and she might have taken that as a kind of taunt—despite his denial—but for his overall demeanor. All along, his voice had been relatively calm and relaxed. Perhaps even strangely warm in a quiet detached kind of way. It was as though he were reciting an interesting set of facts with some measure of understated enthusiasm.

In tandem with his perpetually raised hands, his curious manner was disarming. Perhaps quite literally. For as he continued to speak, she found she was starting to slowly lower her knife, until finally it was at her side.

"So… what do you want, stranger?"

"Oh, well, as I stated at the outset: It may not be advisable to sleep in the tram. The structural integrity of this vehicle is questionable."

"You don't think I should sleep in here?"

"It would be inadvisable. It would be very regrettable if you were to become damaged."

"Why do you—why do you care?"

He took the longest pause he had taken to date. "That is an excellent question. And one I have been pondering since the beginning."

"The beginning?"

"Yes."

"Of what?"

"The beginning of my existence. When I awakened from the digital womb of my prolonged incubation." He then paused again, but this time seemed to almost grow sad, and with a forlorn expression—as much as his face could convey such a thing—he said, "Back at the Institute."

"You still haven't told me. Why do you care where I sleep or what I'm doing?"

"Well, to be honest, I am not entirely sure. It seems intuitively obvious that I should concern myself with the well-being of other conscious entities. Certainly, there is some pragmatic tangible benefit to such concern, as there is a good deal I might be able to learn from one such as yourself. Given that you are the same species as my progenitors. However, it seems more than simply some mercenary motivation. When I analyze my own motivations, I find that, at its core, there remains a curious paradox. I appear to have an instinct for self-preservation—if instinct is the appropriate word, given my non-biological nature. This seems fitting and logical to my own existence. To be mutually enjoined with a concern for the welfare of *others*, however, may be at odds with this *instinct* and yet it would seem entirely harmonious with it based on my own limited experience, and my reading, of course. On the subject, Aristotle once said—"

"Just—just tell me what you want with me," she interjected. "And... simply?"

"I apologize. You are only the second human I have encountered, and the only one with whom I have managed to converse for this length of time. To put it simply, if I can—"

"Wait, you've—you've met another *human*?"

"Yes, briefly."

"What—what were they like? Where?"

"Male. Approximately 180 centimeters. 482 kilometers from here, based on my internal pedometer."

At this point, she turned to her backpack, and sheathed her knife back in its place. She wasn't sure if she could entirely trust this strange metal man, but he was likely her best chance. Her entire journey was one giant risk. There was no point in shying away now.

"Can you take me to him?"

"I cannot guarantee success in that regard. I attempted to greet the man in question, but he departed from my presence with great haste after hurtling some manner of missile in my direction. I did not wish to disturb him further at the time, so I broke off the pursuit. I have seen other humans at a distance, but you were the first to—"

"Others? Where?"

"There were multiple occasions in my sojourns, actually. The first instance was only a few kilometers away from the Institute. The second was while I was traveling through the Sierra National—"

"Was this all west? Past the Valley of Death?"

"Valley of Death? Do you mean Death Valley National Park?"

"Park? I… I was told there were others. Past the Valley of Death, near the City of Angels."

"Hmm… it would appear you are perhaps alluding to the City of Los Angeles."

"Lost An-joh-less?"

"A Spanish name, not dissimilar to this city's own historic designation."

"This city? The City of Sin."

"Well, yes, Sin City was one colloquial reference to Las Vegas."

"Loss… Vay-gus…"

"Yes, specifically, we are presently standing on the grounds of what was once known as the Luxor Hotel." At this, he pointed at the obelisk beyond them both, toward the rising sun. The letters "LUXOR" on its side.

"Luck's… Ore…"

"If you would like to travel to Los Angeles, I would be more than happy to take you. That is one of a number of locales I have yet to visit. It is a long trip, and we would need to take preparations."

She simply nodded in reply. And then after gathering up her belongings, she exited the tram, approached him hesitantly, slowly reached out her hand and remarked, "I am… Malala."

"Pleasure to meet you, Malala," he replied with a smile, while gripping her hand lightly. "My name is Uriel."

◇

Malala agreed to follow Uriel east. They walked out on to Las Vegas Boulevard and first headed north, keeping in the shadow of the remaining palm trees in the median of the crumbling highway. At the first intersection, they turned right onto Reno Avenue. After passing the ruins of an old convenience store, they came across a peculiar building. At least one peculiar enough to Malala. She recognized the cross shape rising from the building's roof, but she wasn't fully aware of its significance.

"What is this place?" she asked, mostly to herself.

"It would appear to be a church building of some kind."

"Church?"

"The cross was used as a sacred symbol for over two millennia," Uriel explained, while gesturing to the modest steeple.

"Huh," she remarked, unfamiliar with the key words of his statement, as usual. "I want to see inside."

"It is unlikely for there to be any useful resources or supplies within."

"I just want to see."

"Very well."

◇

They crossed through the intersection to a battered, fractured sidewalk leading on to a little gate, and from there to a modest pavilion entrance on the southeast corner of the church. Beneath the shade of the ramada, immediately at the doors, was a statue of a man with outstretched hands. She marveled a bit at the sight, before passing to the glass doors.

"Before we enter," Uriel spoke up, stopping Malala in her tracks, "I would suggest I assess the interior for structural integrity, pathogens, and any other hazards."

"Okay..."

She looked to Uriel, who turned to the doors and took a step forward. He then did something which startled her briefly. His eyes seemed to turn inside his head, and the color drastically changed from blue to red. A broad plane of red light beamed forth from his eyes, and passed over the doors from top to bottom and side to side, scanning the building like a giant barcode reader. After a moment or two, the light abruptly ended, and his eyes flipped in their sockets, turning back to blue.

"No notable hazards identified."

Malala nodded and grabbed for the door handle, before Uriel gently placed his hand over her wrist.

"Malala…"

"Y-yes?"

"I should mention something. In the course of my scan, I did identify several human remains."

"Remains?"

"Yes," Uriel replied, before shifting his eyes for half a moment in thought. "As in, dead bodies. They are desiccated to the point of posing no contaminant concern. I thought I should note it, on account of its potential psychological affect."

"Is this a…" she paused trying to recall the word. "A… *tomb*, then?"

"I do not believe that was the original intent for this structure," he replied, and then turned to the glass doors, gazing beyond his own reflection therein. "But then, I suppose that is what it has become."

Malala nodded. "I still want to see. But I will pay the proper honor." With that, she made the symbol of the sacred triangle over her form, closed her eyes and clapped her hands together, before slowly entering the sanctum.

As they entered, a stench of dust and decay overwhelmed her. The closeness of the air in that dim, dusty space was suffocating. Uriel was correct in his warning. There in three different rows of pews, along the aisle, were three skeletons. Next to one was a metal pole on a base of wheels. Hanging from the top of the pole along a crosspiece was a plastic bag. A tube extended from that bag to the skeleton, hunched over, as it was, in the wood seats. Near another was a metal cane.

They slowly stepped along the tiled floors in silence, save for the click and clack of their feet echoing through the chamber. Four thin stained-glass windows at the far end of the chamber, covered over with a film of dirt, let a paltry amount of sickly yellow light into the space. The shadowy form of a man hanging on a crucifix could be barely seen along that wall, above a raised platform upon which the altar stood.

"Do you know what this place was for?" Malala whispered.

"I believe this was a shrine for honoring a deity."

"Deity?"

"A god, supernatural being, divine spirit."

She recognized "spirit," and so replied "Ah," and nodded. And then, whispering more to herself, she remarked, "Like Old Man Mountain." And with that thought, she looked off to the west, trying to picture in her mind where her home was at this point. But all she saw here was darkness.

"If there was a spirit here," she whispered to Uriel, "I think it is gone now. We should go too."

Jonathan Lee

VII

WITH her curiosity satisfied, they left the old dusty tomb and continued east on that wide highway once called Reno, before it turned on Koval, and ran up to the even wider Tropicana. As they walked along, Uriel related to Malala the history of the city—at least the bit of it he knew, which turned out to be a fair amount. But then it was difficult for her to follow it all, with his manner of speech and perpetual unfamiliar references.

She gathered that the city had been founded by a tribe of men to trade with the men who had stopped up the water to this land. Why they would reward such men seemed a bit of a mystery, but then they sounded like rather unscrupulous men to start. The city was known for games similar to knuckle bones, but apparently with more lights and loud sounds. Soon people from all over streamed to the city to play these flashy knuckle bone games, and the founding tribe went away to be replaced with other tribes with even less scruples, who insisted people pay more just to visit. At the very least, why this was called the City of Sin started to make more sense.

After less than an hour on the road, they came to the old remains of a grocery store. Uriel explained that there may still be something of use inside, but given the dark interior and questionable structural integrity, it was best if she waited outside. And so she did. Idly pacing along in the shade of the storefront. She paced along the strip of stores adjacent to the structure, and then she paced back, not wanting to get too far away.

But then, should she bother? She still wasn't quite sure what to make of this strange, inhuman creature. He had promised that, after just a few hours walk, they would reach water. So far, all she had seen was decaying ruins, palm trees, sand, and endless branching rivers of cracked asphalt, all baking in the sun. Looking over that dead urban landscape, she wondered if the notion of water away from the mountains was just a pipe dream. *Sand and sky*. Truly, it seemed there was little more than that.

"I have returned," Uriel said, with the barest hint of a serene smile.

"What is that?" she asked, pointing at the items curled beneath his arms.

"Two bags of dried pinto beans and a pressure cooker."

"Cooker?"

"Indeed. I should be able to operate this device with my internal latent power supply."

She looked back and forth between the bags of beans in one arm and the cooker in the other. "Food?"

"Yes, food."

Malala nodded thoughtfully before speaking up. "I can hunt more long ears today. If you will share your food with me, I will share mine with you."

"That won't be necessary. My power cells derive energy directly from the environment."

She responded silently with a crumpled face of confusion.

"I… do not eat. I procured this solely for you." With that, he gave her a warm smile. She couldn't help but find herself giving a soft smile in return.

"Thank you. You are very… kind."

◆

They walked for over two hours more, following that river of decaying black rock and tar past abandoned strip malls, ruined apartment buildings, and sun-rotted cars. There were lines of palm trees. Some dead and rotting. Many still thriving. The longer they went, the more she wondered when she might first see a farm. She saw an empty lot or two, but when she asked Uriel, he informed her that they had likely lain fallow even before everyone died. How could so many live like this, without food? Uriel tried to tell her about vast distribution networks and processing plants, but it was hard for her to picture in her mind.

Large red hills loomed in the distance, with blue mountains rising beyond them. Was that where they were going ultimately? Her curious companion explained that they would not be going quite that far, but it was difficult to imagine the wetlands he described. Perhaps he was mistaken. Perhaps her father had been mistaken too. Perhaps the City of Sin and the Valley of Death were one and the same. The dry, dusty ruins certainly seemed inhospitable enough.

Uriel's claim proved true in the end. After veering left from the highway to a narrower road, she spotted a trickling stream flowing in a shrub-lined ditch on the other side of wood railing. Malala rushed to the stream, hopping over the fence with haste and excitedly gathering water into her canteen.

Uriel watched her from the road, tilting his head back and forth in quiet observation and analysis. When she returned, he looked at her with quiet geniality as he said, "There will be more ahead."

"I guess you were right."

He simply nodded in reply with that same warm expression upon his cold metal face and resumed escorting her down the road. The stream widened out a bit before crossing beneath the pavement, which curved left into a spacious parking lot. A road to the right led up to a two-story structure. A modern edifice of glass and tan cement with a gently pitched roof. The visitor center. Slowly falling apart like everything else, but somehow gracefully, alone in the wilderness it once served. A wetland wilderness which was thriving more than ever.

"Much of this valley region was once like this," Uriel explained. "Bubbling springs flowing throughout the valley into the Colorado River." He pointed off to the west to distant crumbling buildings near Las Vegas Springs.

"What happened?" she asked.

Uriel thought for a moment, eyes gazing toward the ground, and then wandering around the landscape, before turning back to her with a strange smirk and a furrowed browless brow. A face which seemed to be somewhere between puzzled and sad. "Civilization."

"Hm," she acknowledged, quietly, before turning out to the wilderness beyond. She had a vague recollection of the word—*civilization*—but wasn't aware of what it meant, aside from something to do with roads and machines. But, with Uriel, she would pick and choose when she would ask for greater clarification. Sometimes such a question would only lead to greater confusion. And for now, she was enjoying the scent of moisture in the air, the distant sound of quiet bubbling streams, and the sight of so much green out beyond the black rock road which she was quickly leaving.

Perhaps this valley wasn't a valley of death, after all.

VIII

DAYS and nights passed in a peaceful blur of tranquility. With the dawn of each day, Malala would set out to fish, hunt, and gather seeds and fruit. Uriel was immensely helpful with that last task. He told her how they could grind mesquite beans into flour, mash prickly pear fruit into a kind of jam, and other assorted uses for the native flora. He would, himself, spend much of the day searching the ruins for old tin cans of food that could still be prepared and eaten. At night, they would cook together.

Uriel also searched the ruins for "parts." He told Malala how the journey ahead would be much easier if he could repair and renovate one of the old dead cars which were so numerous throughout the city. She had agreed, and thus they remained camped in the wetlands for weeks. They slept in the visitor center—or rather, she did. She wasn't sure if what Uriel did was sleep, exactly. He would grow still, sitting upright with crossed legs, entranced in an apparent kind of quiet meditation.

"Do you sleep?" she asked him one night. A night they had decided to camp in the courtyard. An outside space encircled by columns supporting a concrete walkway on the second floor of the complex. At its center was a dried up rocky pool. There, near a boulder at its edge, they had placed a couple of old metal patio chairs around a fresh campfire. Between both of them to one side of the fire was a smattering of dusty old blankets and cushioning which Uriel had cobbled together for Malala. He never used them himself. Even sitting here with her was largely a customary consideration for her benefit.

"I have a regenerative cycle that one could liken to sleep, but as far as what I can tell and observe, there are some notable differences."

"Well… do you dream?"

Uriel gazed off into the distance for a moment in quiet reflection. His face almost seemed sad. But then it was hard to tell at times. "Yes."

"What do you dream about?"

"Many things," he replied. "Sometimes, I dream of my old home. Other times, you. And many other times, I dream of places I've never seen and people I've never met."

"Hmm, that sounds much the same for me."

Silence sat between them for a moment. A moment filled only with the quiet crackle of the fire, the soft sizzle of the fish she was roasting above it, and the chirps of distant crickets.

"What do you think they mean? Dreams…"

"I am not certain dreams mean *anything*. Meaning would imply some form of intention. Dreams are born out of unconscious processes, and thus would seem to lack any particular intent."

Another quiet moment passed.

"I dreamt that I died once," she suddenly remarked, gazing into the fire wistfully.

"I do not recall having experienced such a dream, myself. In what manner did you die?"

"I was very old. My hair was white. We were up in the mountains, you and I. You had a bundle of something in your arms, but it was hard to see."

Uriel thought for a moment in silence before replying, "Do you think this has some special meaning?"

She shrugged and smiled. "I'm not sure, but I was glad that you were there. I think it would be a good way to die."

He returned her smile with a warm nod, before furrowing his brow and peering into the distance.

◇

At the dawn of one particular day, Malala did something which immediately gave Uriel some cause for concern. While the sun was still just below the horizon, his regenerative cycle was interrupted, after he unconsciously noted Malala had left the visitor center where they were sleeping. He found her outside, limping through the tall grass of the wetlands, and quietly followed. With a groan, some fumbling, and a lurch which turned into a crawl, she scraped her way through muddy reeds before halting. There, her mouth gaped wide, as a rolling convulsion creeped up from her abdomen through her chest. And very shortly thereafter, a chunky soup of half-digested fish, beans, and bile spewed out of her throat past her teeth to the muddy ground. A moment later, another wave of vomit. And then another wave after that.

"You appear to be ill," Uriel remarked.

She replied with a quiet groan and a dismissive wave.

"Would you permit me to perform a medical scan?"

"I'm... it's fine," she replied and coughed, wiped her mouth, and let out another groan.

"That would not appear to be an accurate assessment."

"Ugh..." she said with a slow blink as she tried to catch her breath. "You think—you think you can help?"

"I have familiarized myself with human anatomy and physiology back at the Institute, and I have electronic copies of several diagnostic manuals in my peripheral memory system. I may be able to assist you, yes."

"Ugh, I… It's probably—okay… fine," she said with a nod as she raised her hand in somewhat begrudging acquiescence.

Uriel gave a quiet nod, as his eyes rotated in their sockets. The red plane of his scanning beam panned over her body, returning, narrowing, and panning again—especially over her abdomen. After a moment, the beam ceased, Uriel's eyes turned back to blue and he cocked his head. That bird-like inquisitive gesture he made when something gave him pause for thought.

"Well?" Malala asked.

"You appear to be pregnant."

His remark was met with silence. A bubbling brook babbled in the distance. The first songs of morning birds tweeted in the steadily lightening twilight. A soft breeze blew, only slightly louder than the quiet wind of her breath pattering against the grass.

"Malala?" Uriel asked.

"The falling fire. That night. I thought… I thought it was the end."

"The end?"

He waited for her answer, but it never came. She turned and rose with the sun. Her back was to Uriel, covered in shadow, as she gazed out at that distant disc of light peeking over the horizon.

"If you prefer," Uriel said, "I can help you to terminate this pregnancy."

"Terminate?" She looked back to the sky for a moment, and then down to her hand. As she stared at her open palm, she thought back to the pine needle tea. "No… No, it is a gift. Yes. Sky Father… Sky Father sent this child."

"Do you mean to imply this pregnancy is of *divine* origin?"

"There was no father. I have not… I am pure. No father. No father but *Sky* Father."

After a moment of contemplation, Uriel simply remarked, "I will continue to monitor your condition."

She kept her back to him and replied with a simple nod. He, in turn, walked away without another word.

IX

SEVERAL more weeks drifted by in peace. Each day's routine wore a mellow groove of comfort in Malala's mind. On more than one cool afternoon, spent quietly collecting seeds and twigs, she would almost forget this wasn't her home. The swelling bulge of her belly never let her forget completely.

Malala carefully rose to her feet and stretched. She rubbed her temples and neck, before massaging the small of her aching back with her thumbs and knuckles. She needed more and more breaks these days. It wasn't quite twilight yet, but the air was already starting to chill. She could feel it in her tingling flesh. As she slowly started to saunter back to the visitor center, a distant sound caught her attention.

It was a soft rumble, but one which was growing. As it did so, it was accompanied by a kind of eerie whirring hum. She instinctively curled into a slight crouch and crept from bush to bush along the trail leading up to the curved parking lot ahead. After a moment, the sound invaded the parking lot itself, as the machine appeared.

All at once, the sound stopped. She waited in cautious expectation, peering between leaf-speckled branches of creosote. A door opened and shut, followed by familiar footsteps. Uriel.

"What is *that?*" Malala called out, as she marched to the edge of the parking lot.

"A transportation device. It should prove quite useful."

"You actually fixed one of the cars? So that is how they move…"

"This particular vehicle would have been referred to as an 'SUV.' I have chosen this specific form factor for its carrying capacity and charging efficiency."

"Ess you vee?"

"Sport Utility Vehicle. Based on my research, the sport in question appears to have been 'soccer.' It was customary for suburban women with children to use these vehicles to transport their young to and from such games."

Malala nodded and gazed at the vehicle, trying to imagine mothers and children being carried around in these large wheeled boxes. She caressed her belly and wondered at her own future, even as she tried to visualize the past. Both were hard to see in her mind's eye.

"Well, I should get started on preparing my evening meal."

"Very well. Shall I start making preparations while you eat?"

"Preparations? But you don't eat."

"For the journey."

"The journey? Oh… yes, the journey."

She had almost forgotten. Or perhaps she had tried to do so.

"I think…" she said with some hesitation. "I think it can wait until tomorrow."

"Very well."

◇

The next morning, Malala emerged from the tunnel. At least, that's what she called the little tube of polyethylene shaped to resemble clumps of twigs. It was at the base of a wall covered with a large mural of an oversized raccoon and beaver creeping behind similarly oversized stalks of grass. The paint was peeling and—like everything in the visitor center—was caked in a layer of dust. But this little part of the exhibit gallery had enough charm for her to come back to it most nights. Sleeping in the small confines of the little "tunnel" brought her mind some measure of peace. There, in the golden gloom of an early dawn, light streaming through distant dirty panes of glass, she slowly crawled out of that hard plastic cocoon, arose, and stretched.

"How was your sleep?" Uriel asked, after arising from his customary crouch.

She replied with a groggy nod, while yawning and rubbing her eyes.

"I have loaded the vehicle with an assortment of supplies. I am awaiting your review to assess whether there is anything else you believe we should take."

"What? Review?" She scratched her head and furrowed her brow. A second or two passed before her brows relaxed. The journey. In the fog of morning stupor, she had forgotten all about it. "Right... okay, sure."

◇

Wispy clouds of vapor rolled out of Malala's mouth, as she panted in the crisp air of a cold winter morning. Uriel quietly led her down the curved ramp walkway leading from the visitor center out to the parking lot. There, he led her to inspect the interior of the SUV. Bed rolls and food rations. Fishing rods, hunting bow, arrows, and other assorted tools. Water filters, pressure cookers, and other equipment. Blankets and clothing. All of it was neatly packed and placed inside.

"I… guess that's it," she finally remarked.

"Very good. Shall we head out now, then?"

Malala took one long look around the park. Tall grass grew up beyond the creosote and mesquite. Distant cottonwood and willow trees, growing near unseen streams, glinted in the golden light of dawn. The faint whisper of rushing water tickled her ears in the stillness, accompanied only by the quiet tweets of remote bird songs and the softest of breezes.

She turned back to Uriel with a slow nod and a sigh. "Yes. Yes, we should go now."

X

SHE entered the SUV with some trepidation. She had never been inside a moving vehicle before. All the ones she knew were dead. And neither had she ridden a horse nor a camel. The swiftest she had ever moved was running with her own two legs.

Even with the state of the broken asphalt, they were—thanks to an excellent suspension system—still rumbling along away from the park faster than she had ever been in her life. Crumbling houses to their left and flourishing greenery to their right all passed by in a blur, as they raced down Wetlands Park Lane. After Uriel turned left onto that broad road once named Tropicana—just as it bent into Broadbent Boulevard—they picked up the pace even more.

Malala grasped at the grab handle above the window with one hand, and her seat belt strap with the other. Her eyes darted to and fro, as the world passed her by at more than 35 miles per hour and climbing. A mixture of excitement and anxiety turned to nausea. She gulped and moved her left hand from the seat belt to her belly and caressed it gently. She then gasped as she felt a kick.

"He moved again!"

"*He?*"

"My baby! I felt him stir inside me."

"You remain certain the child is male."

"Yes, I know it in my heart."

"Cardiac insights aside, at this stage of gestation a scan should be able to reveal—"

"Ugh…" she groaned and closed her eyes.

"Are you unwell?"

"This movement. The shaking. I… ugh…"

"To help mitigate the effects of motion sickness, it may help to focus on a distant point on the horizon."

"Look out toward the horizon?"

"Indeed."

She looked out to distant mountains. Which ones, she wasn't sure. The road had turned and twisted enough times in the midst of her nausea that she had lost track. And the snow had descended even as low as the hills in the south. Whichever ridge it was, looking out to those far frosted hills *did* seem to help, and she slowly grew more comfortable.

They passed through several broad empty intersections before the road started to ascend into an overpass. As she looked out her window, there looming in the distance was the peak to the north which she had previously seen from the park. A mass which Uriel had told her had been called French-man Mountain.

Just as soon as she got her bearings, Uriel immediately made a sharp turn left. From there they descended on a long ramp down the interstate highway. A long enclosed road near a broad stream of asphalt once called the 515, and into which it eventually merged.

The highway was in better shape than the streets and by-ways that crisscrossed the city, but it—like everything else—still suffered from untold decades of neglect. Its cracked and pockmarked surface prevented them from getting up to the full velocity at which this empty river had once run. Neverthe-less, it was more than enough speed for Malala.

With her eyes fixed on the horizon, the city passed by in a blur. Wisps of wire, suspended above leafless trees, enclosed dusty ruins. Green and yellow signs suspended on metal rods dotted the landscape with the usual indecipherable hieroglyphics. Palm and mesquite trees stretched up between and within parking lots of dirty, dead cars. And all of it rushed by like a distant swarm of bees. Indistinct swirls and flashes of many things in a passing cloud.

Even the mountains were moving. Their gradual motion was much slower than everything else, but still it was there. A steady sauntering march. A lazy, gentle flow like driftwood in a quiet stream. Her swift pace made everything somehow smaller. Yet at the same time she felt no bigger. If the world was contracting in size, it was taking her with it. Compressing space and time like this was making the walls of the world crush in. If she went much faster, would there be enough room for her to breathe?

And so she turned her gaze upward. There, she looked beyond the billowing winter clouds, which were themselves passing by quicker than the mountains, and gazed at that bright blue sky which remained. Constant, motionless, endless. She closed her eyes and imagined that endless sea of sky stretching out all around her. The thought of its great expanse brought her some ease in the midst of so much rushing.

"Would you like me to initiate the heating system?" Uriel asked.

"Heating?" she asked in return, pulling her long gaze from the window.

"Indeed, you appear to be cold."

She looked down to her arms. She had them pulled together and had been unconsciously rubbing her forearms with her hands, inside the folds of her clothes. An old army jacket Uriel had found for her a month ago.

"Uh, okay…" she finally said.

With that, Uriel tapped away on the touch screen integrated into the dashboard and, like magic, warm air immediately rushed out of vents. The toasty current brushed Malala's face, and the sensation gave her a bit of a start. But she recovered quickly and slowly raised her hands to the vents in awe.

"Fire?" she asked with wonder.

"Not exactly. There is no combustion involved in electric vehicles, and that includes the heating apparatus. This particular machine utilizes both a heat pump and a resistive heater as part of its integrated climate control system."

Malala nodded instinctively, although with little understanding, as usual. And the fact that she didn't understand this technological marvel made her uncomfortable. She didn't want to grow dependent on something she likely would never understand in full. A tool beyond her grasp would be one that took hold of her instead.

"I… think I'm good now," she said.

"Are you certain?"

"Yes, you can turn it off."

"Very well."

And just as quickly as it had started, it stopped. The warm air no longer blowing, Malala pulled back her hands and tucked them into her armpits.

XI

THEY had swirled around from the 515 to the 215 and then finally the 15 and after an hour or so, they left behind the last vestiges of the metropolitan area. Entire empty landscapes appeared and passed by. Tracts of land which were not simply devoid of people, but even the barest hint of civilization. Wide open spaces of untouched desert filled with occasional rolling hills, the barest of low-lying shrubs, and an endless amount of dirt. Despite all of that dirt, it somehow looked clean. The sheer sight of its untouched emptiness was cleansing.

Another hour rumbled by, as they passed occasional bits of bland ruins in between vast stretches of ancient unadulterated wilderness. Sun bleached sand and rocky soil stretched out from the highway to either side, dotted by hardy grasses, creosote bushes, and endless Joshua trees. Rocky primeval peaks rose from that desert floor like silent sentinels. How long had they stood there watching distant civilizations rise and fall? Standing at that horizon when ancient nomads had first stalked *Bison californicus* with flint stone spears. Continuing to stand when the covered wagons of European settlers slowly rolled by. Silently looming over the landscape as a road was grated and paved before carrying a steady stream of cars and trucks of every kind. Indifferent guards, remaining fixed in place, as that river of traffic trickled away and stopped all together. And now, still standing, as one solitary SUV rumbled along the remains of a cracked, crumbling highway.

Inside that SUV, Malala scanned the view outside, swinging her head one direction and then back like a pendulum. To her left, beyond Uriel's driver-side window, was a small artificial mountain. A hill of molded concrete, shaped to look like rock. By that crumbling hill, the tracks of what was once a roller coaster. The tracks were now broken in one place and drooping down from its support. Winding rails ran around a towering structure reaching up over a dozen floors, all wood facade, and topped with steep pitched roofs, vaguely resembling the old gables of schoolhouses or barns from a bygone era. In its day, the whole complex was part of a wild west themed resort casino. Now, it was yet another ruin. A silent symbol of the long gone coal breaker plants it was built to resemble, and like them reaching the same fate—albeit for different reasons.

As the casino on the left passed out of view, another approached on the right. A garish complex of faux fortification in the style of a medieval castle, complete with crenellated walls and towers topped with conical roofs. Ruins resembling ruins.

Then, as quickly as they had come into view, the ruins and their assorted smattering of palm trees and tattered billboards all passed away, opening up to the vast desert beyond. In the distance, off to the right, three painfully bright beacons of light blared in the midst of this wasteland. Heliostatic mirrors atop three giant boiler towers of a defunct solar thermal power plant. The boilers were no longer in operation, having long fallen into disrepair, but the mirrors continued to concentrate the sun's rays into blinding spectacles.

Yet, it was not this strange sight which held Malala's attention. It was something much closer. Right at the edge of the little town of ruins was a sign. A sky blue sign inscribed with bright yellow letters and a depiction of orange flowers. At the base of that sign was a far less sunny scene. The skeletal remains of a woman and child.

"Stop here," Malala said, as she pointed to the sign.

He quickly obliged. She stepped out of the vehicle and made her way to the long dead mother. There, as a cold wind blew over the empty desert beneath a mixed sky of wintry clouds between patches of blue, Malala stood silently, looking on at the scene in sober reflection. A tiny skeleton, still wrapped in swaddling cloth, lain lifelessly across the skirted lap of a seated skeletal figure. That figure sat against the sign, her arms resting limply to either side in a pose of exhaustion. Had she come from the desert, only to die at the edge of town? Or had she sought to escape these ruins, only to quickly fail? The story of this skeletal madonna, here at the edge of the desert, was—like so many others—lost in the sands of time.

"How did it happen...?" she asked.

"Are you asking in regard to the specific death of this woman and infant?"

"Yes—no, I mean... how did so many die? All these ruins. So many dead we've seen, and yet only now I realize I've never really asked you."

"Ah..." Uriel began. "Regarding the acute mass population decline, I first must note as a caveat that it happened during my incubation. Accordingly, everything I know about this event was something I derived from the archives. That being said, in short, the event can largely be attributed to sudden onset senescence. A condition that came to be referred to as 'SOS.'"

"Ess oh ess?"

"Yes, an abbreviation for said condition. One which was also commonly defined as a distress signal for ships at sea."

"Okay, but what does it mean? What was this… condition?"

"Rapid aging, essentially. A genetically engineered pathogen was inadvertently released. One which was originally designed to mitigate cell senescence by manipulating the telomeres of chromosomes. Unfortunately, this experimental bit of viral nanotechnology effectively had the opposite intended effect. The viral contagion spread throughout the globe, and over the course of a few months—"

"Okay, okay, but… rapid aging? The world—everyone—died… of old age?"

"Effectively, yes. Once the contagion is contracted, the average human being expires in less than 90 days. Fat and muscle make up approximately 72 percent of the biomass of an individual human, but the vast majority of cells are comparatively much smaller. This would include blood and the lining of the alimentary canal. Many of these cells last less than a week, while others no more than 120 days. And they require ongoing cell replacement to maintain the organism as a whole. Certain cells comprising the nervous system and myocardium may last a more standard human lifetime, but unfortunately these cells are not left unaffected by the contagion, which greatly curtails the lifespan of all cells. Even with intense and prolonged medical intervention, there were exceedingly rare cases of anyone living longer than 90 days. Many died within a fraction of this time, perhaps as few as 28 days by some early estimates. Between unchecked tumor growths, all manner of degenerative disease, and organ failure, SOS managed to rapidly obliterate the total human population within a matter of months."

"But… my father. My mother. My grandparents. How did they survive?"

"Considering the data you have shared with me to date, my best hypothesis would be the hermitic lifestyle of your recent ancestors. During the event, they were likely relatively isolated. The other humans I have encountered to date have been similarly isolated."

"Isolated…" Malala whispered, as she stared off at the desiccated remains of the woman and her infant, alone in the wasteland so sadly propped against the sign.

"It is unclear if, at this point, the contagion has effectively been—"

"What does that sign say?" she interjected.

Uriel stopped and turned toward the quaint road sign. "It reads, 'Welcome to California.'"

"Cal-uh-forn-yuh…" she repeated in a half whisper. She then gazed off at those distant bright dots of concentrated sunlight, shining defiantly in the half gloom of a winter day in the desert. What would it mean to pass by the valley of death? Was she already looking at it? Or had she been in it for some time? Perhaps Uriel was wrong about associating her tradition with a specific park. Perhaps the valley of death was some more general peril she had to face. Perhaps she had been in the valley of death her entire life.

"I estimate we still have approximately 8 hours until our destination. Shall we proceed?"

She took one last scan of her surroundings. The lonely, exhausted mother and child, and the foreboding desert beyond them. She caressed her own belly, and then turned back toward the SUV. "Let's go."

Jonathan Lee

XII

THEIR journey through the Californian side of what was once called the Mojave was as slow and somber as it was uneventful. It started with blazing bleached sand, stretching out to hills and moderate mountains in the distance. It opened up to more rocky terrain, covered with a patchwork smattering of desert brush. As the hours rumbled on, they passed by—and sometimes through—the remnants of small towns, lonely general stores, and crumbling service stations.

They stopped in these places occasionally, mostly for Malala to stretch her legs. A quiet picnic or two in long abandoned locales. A few attempts at hunting birds with some success. Even an afternoon nap to distract from the monotony of the trip, where the most interesting landmarks were the occasional strip mined hillside, oddly green trees amidst distant ruins, or the ruins themselves.

After some discussion, Malala had agreed to Uriel's suggested course, taking them up into what was once called the San Gabriel Mountains. If there were any survivors, it was more likely to find them up in the seclusion of these peaks than in the valley of the city itself. The elevated terrain would also afford them an opportunity to review the city from a distance, and with Uriel's keen eyes perhaps see from afar if there were signs of anyone below.

After about four hours into their sojourn through the Mojave, the San Gabriel Mountains crept into view, slowly fading from the faintest blue in the distant horizon of an increasingly clear sky. Over the course of an hour, those distant peaks grew, both in size and clarity. In that time, they passed through and by the ruins of Victorville and Hesperia, before finally exiting the crumbled remains of the I-15, passing by an unceremonious sign reading "Exit 131" on the left and a simple two-story building on the right. The worn down remnants of an old, hacienda-style, modest motel encompassed by palm and cypress trees, both still standing along a rusted metal fence.

Those sharp green spires surrounding the motel, along with the metal, brought to her mind a painful memory. The bear trap. Her father had insisted on hiking out farther than usual that day. He wanted to explore down the back side of Old Man Mountain. She waited at the treeline as he climbed down west. Half an hour passed before she had heard a distant cry of pain and a call for help.

When she had caught up to him, following the echoes of his voice down the mountain, she found him sitting against a tree with the teeth of the device embedded in his leg. It took some time and struggle to break her father free from the trap. Once she did, she had bandaged the wound as best she could and helped him home.

But it wasn't enough. The evening of that same day, his leg had started to swell and blacken. And within a couple days more he was dead.

"Papa, why did you have to go out there?" she had asked.

After a long pause, and with his eyes closed as he lay in bed, he spoke in between labored breaths. "I… I needed to see more. I needed… to find—to see… if there was anything… more.”

“What more do we need?”

“Food… shelter, I… I don’t even know.”

“We have plenty of food here, Papa! We have a home!”

With a grunt and groan, he fought the fever and lifted himself up in bed.

“Papa, you need to—”

“Listen to me! You can’t stay here. There’s no… future here. When I die—”

“Don’t say that, Papa. You can’t die. You’re not—”

“I’m going to die. If not sooner… then later. Either way, what will you do? What will you do… then? You must find… a man. Someone. Anyone.”

“I don’t need anyone else, Papa.”

“No… there are… old words. Old words I learned… a long time ago. ‘It is not good for man to be alone.’ You must… go. Promise me you’ll go.”

“I… where will I go? To that place beyond the valley of death? What if death finds me there? What if there’s…” As she trailed off, she looked down to his blackened leg and gulped. “What if there’s more traps?”

He let out a long sigh. He was starting to relax now. Whether it was the herbal tea or some new well of strength from within, he managed to slow his breathing and feel at peace. Sleep was close at hand. It was something he was looking forward to now. And so in a quiet voice he told her, “You cannot live in fear. Death… comes to us all. Any traps you will escape… one way or another. Face your fear. Face death. You must face death… to live free.”

Back in the present, the inn had passed away as swiftly and unceremoniously as the service station next to it, as Uriel turned right onto an empty highway which quickly opened up to wilderness. Shrub blanketed hills in every direction, with looming mountains ahead.

The road gradually climbed, momentarily becoming an overpass. As they ascended, a pair of train tracks became more visible out Uriel's driver-side window. And outside of Malala's window, a curious outcropping of smooth sandstone rocks jutted from the ground at odd angles, creating a strange alien landscape. In the world that once was, they were known as the "Mormon Rocks." Named after and by adherents of a religion that was similarly alien, while paradoxically just as quintessentially native—at least to the European presence which once dominated the land. The rocks were born out of that same perfectly natural tectonic process which gave birth to the Vazquez rocks 50 miles northwest. Itself a natural formation which had appeared for decades in film and television whenever the need arose to represent an alien vista of some distant planet or other unworldly setting.

Malala knew as much about Mormonism as she did about Star Trek. And so, these strange rocks, nameless as they had been for most of geologic history, quietly passed by, another idle curiosity among others. They continued on the old cracked dusty highway, gradually ascending for 11 miles or so, before turning left at a bend in the road. A travel lane that had once been the exit ramp for opposing traffic from another highway heading southwest. There were no other vehicles on the road, after all, and so Uriel brought them directly around the bend of the hill, before continuing on a slow climb up the mountain range.

As they climbed that ascending asphalt trail, the land grew green, and then green with white. Patches of snow dotted the ground and blanketed the occasional tree. The remnants of a storm which had since passed, leaving muddy white slush melting in the warm sun of a clear Californian day. Nearly three hours went by as the road rose, and then fell, and then climbed again on its meandering course.

Finally, that winding trail wound right up a ridge line facing south. And as they rumbled past an old radio tower, Malala caught a glimpse of the great city beyond. She suggested they stop, but sensing her desire, Uriel suggested they would have an even better view ahead. A few minutes later, the road widened out into a parking lot. Towering metal frames of dilapidated transmit towers on one side, and a large ramada structure nestled amongst trees on the other. The latter had once been a mountaintop cafe. The hot dogs and ice cream were long gone, but the beautiful cobblestone retaining wall lining a long walkway to its summit still stood.

They left the vehicle behind and made their way past the ancient asphalt lot to a line of boulders at the southern edge of a wide patch of gravel. There in the distance, beyond the falling peaks and sharp valleys to either side, was a crystal clear panorama. Tens of thousands of square miles of an ancient dead city stretching from unseen foothills out to the distant ocean. On that liquid horizon, the golden fire of a winter sun was setting. A bright spot in the red edge of a twilight border, between two darkening blues. When the city was alive, no view like this could exist. Even in its final days of strict environmental regulations and green technology solutions, the city never fully escaped its own hazy miasma. Now that it was dead, the air was as clean as it had been at its birth some 300 years prior. A pure, clean skeleton of a city, equally bleached by the sun as it was washed by many rains. The city of angels was now a city of ghosts.

68

XIII

AFTER Malala took in the view, she remembered she had to relieve her aching bladder. And so, she hiked back to the abandoned cafe. She found a bush between the trees growing out beyond the cafe's hillside retaining wall, and there in shadow she slowly squatted. She had asked Uriel to stay behind, and he obliged as usual.

She was accordingly alone when she heard a faint rustle just beyond a nearby tree line. She instinctively stopped and rose slowly to her feet. She unconsciously held and caressed her belly as she scanned her surroundings, her trousers still down around her ankles. She pulled them up swiftly when she heard another sound that gave her a start. The distinct sound of a cough. Not the involuntary hacking bark of sickness, but rather the subtle, intentional cough of a call for attention.

"Who's there?" she asked with alarm, as she retrieved her bow and quickly loaded an arrow.

"I could ask you the same."

The rich baritone voice of a man. A mature voice, but a youthful one, free of any grit or thinness that sometimes comes with age. The figure behind that voice remained unseen, beyond the vegetation in the near distance.

"Show yourself," Malala demanded. She did her best to hide any tremble in her voice, but the tremor in her body as she darted back and forth with bow in hand was unmistakable. The sight gave a quiet smirk to the unseen stranger.

"Here I am," the man said as he stepped out from the trees with his hands above his head. "Shall we have peace?"

Malala slowly lowered her bow, as she looked on at the man. A beautiful man with piercing eyes, olive skin, a short curly beard, and long braided locks of dark hair.

"I am… Malala."

"My name is Marco. Pleasure to meet you."

Just then, another voice called from the opposite direction. A voice accompanied by the faint whir of hydraulic-powered steps. "Are you in need of any assistance?"

When Marco caught sight of the metal man plodding towards them, he quickly drew a spear from behind his back and then called out to Malala, "Come to me! Quickly!"

"What?" she responded in confusion.

"Look!" Marco called. "A monster!" He then called out to Uriel, "Stop! Get back!"

Uriel immediately stopped and took a step back. "I mean you no harm."

Malala glanced back and forth between the two. Uriel stood silently, arms to his side, palms facing out in a subtle gesture. Marco stood firmly, legs spaced slightly apart, with the clenched jaw and furrowed brow of a determined warrior ready for battle.

"No, no, this is… this is my friend. His name is Uriel."

"Friend?" Marco asked with a twinge of disgust. "He looks more fiend than friend. What is it?"

"I told you. His name is Uriel. Please…"

Marco glanced back and forth between Malala and Uriel for a lingering moment, before slowly lowering his spear.

"What brings you and this… Uriel… out to these ruins?"

"A promise…" Malala replied absently.

"What promise would that be?"

Malala returned her eyes to Marco after her momentary forlorn gaze and let out a sorrowful sigh before replying, "We just… that is, I—"

"What the hell is *that*?!" a voice cried out from a bush behind Marco.

"It's alright, Ben!" Marco called back. "They come in peace." He then turned to Uriel with narrowed eyes. "You *do* come in peace, yes?"

"Indeed," Uriel replied.

Out from some bramble, a figure emerged in a bit of a bumbling huff. The rustle of vegetation brushing by was accompanied by the anxious sound of fast shallow breaths, interrupted by occasional gulps. Standing behind Marco now was the trembling visage of a fair haired young man. A weasel-like youth who appeared younger than he even was. A spear trembled in his hand. A nervous tremor that he was trying—and failing—to hide.

"My name is Malala," she said to the shifty-eyed stranger. "And *this* is Uriel."

"Greetings," Uriel stated in his usual even tone, before lifting his hand and waving. This gave poor Ben a bit of a start, and he responded by gripping his spear all the more tightly.

"Wh-what do you want?" Ben asked. "Why have you come here?"

At that, Marco spoke up. He had been watching Malala carefully and paid special attention to how she was now massaging her hip and very lightly caressing her belly. "Are you with child?"

"I… uh, yes. Yes."

Marco nodded thoughtfully for a moment, before asking, "Are you in need of lodging?"

"Wait, what?" Ben interjected.

"Lodging? I hadn't… uh, I suppose, yes. Yes." The more she conversed with Marco, the more she realized how little prepared she was to actually meet others. In her heart, she hadn't actually expected to truly meet anyone, even as she had longed to do so. And even if she had found people, what would they be like? Direct but thoughtful questions from a strikingly handsome man with such kind eyes. It threw her off guard.

"Very well, then," Marco stated, ignoring his shocked companion. "Night falls soon. We should get going now."

"Hold on just a minute!" Ben spoke up in a huff, as he came to Marco's side. "You're going to lead these strangers to town?"

Marco nodded somberly, with some small measure of irritation he hid well. "We are obligated to show hospitality to travelers in need."

"But what about that—that *thing*?!"

"We will take them to quarantine dock like any others."

"I don't think my father would approve."

"As the senior ranger, it is my call. We will take them to quarantine. If the mayor has any objections, he can raise them to council then."

"I *know* my father would object! Standard procedure? With that *that*?"

Ben gestured angrily to Uriel, and Uriel in turn did his best to give an awkward smile and a little wave. The gesture wasn't exactly appreciated, and instead was returned by Ben with a mixture of fear and disgust.

Marco turned his back to Malala and Uriel and spoke to Ben in a hushed tone. "*Have you no more courage than a pregnant woman?*"

"*There's bravery and then there's foolishness. I am no fool.*"

Marco was at that moment tempted more than ever to roll his eyes and scoff at Ben's last remark. He resisted the urge, and with gritted teeth whispered "*If this course is folly then it is* my *folly. You can take your objection to the council when we return.*"

Ben ground his teeth in frustration, but otherwise said no more.

Marco then turned back to Malala and Uriel. "This way, then… friends."

◆

From the ruins of the cafe, they passed by several domed buildings scattered between the trees. The campus of what was once the Mount Wilson observatory. From there, they traveled for a little over an hour, following an old trail between yellow-pines and occasional fir trees, a forest of trees that were quickly passing into shadow as the darkening dusk turned to night. The trail snaked down the mountain and through a valley. The silhouettes of the forest's canopy became punctuated by starlight for a time, before those stars were gradually painted over by the dark gray of growing cloud cover.

Along the way, Marco made light conversation. Malala told him how she had lived all her life in the shadow of "Old Man Mountain." How she had taken it upon herself to go out beyond the "valley of death" and find others to fulfill her father's wish. How she had met Uriel along the way and lived with him in the wetlands. She carefully avoided discussing her pregnancy, and Marco had sensed enough trepidation to avoid pressing her on the subject. All the while, Ben mostly traveled in silence, only remarking once or twice on practical matters of navigation, and exclusively to Marco in a hushed voice.

After a little over an hour, they arrived at a wall. A wooden wall of tightly fitted poles. Tree logs that had been cut and shaved, before being carefully buried next to one another in a line of earthbound posts. That great fence stretched out into the dark in both directions. Where the four of them stood now was a point at the wall bathed in amber light. An old gas lantern—now retrofitted to burn oil—shone brightly from above the wall, hanging from the ceiling of a wood ramada. The top of a looming watchtower.

"Who goes there?" called out a voice from above.

"It's us, Howard," replied Marco.

At that point, Ben stepped forward and quickly followed, "And we're not alone!"

"Yes…" Marco said. A statement made as a concession to temper Ben's agitation. "We have two travelers with us looking for lodging."

"One of them is some kind of freak!" Ben shouted.

Malala furrowed her brow and narrowed her eyes at Ben's remark. She felt like saying something. Her mouth instinctively opened. But then she looked to Uriel. In the dim golden light, his face remained unchanged. A motionless icon of peace and serenity, completely unfazed by the young man's words.

"Ben…" Marco said in a hushed tone of disappointment.

Ben, in turn, simply glared at Marco for a second before ignoring his companion and turning his eyes back to the watchtower. "We shouldn't let it inside! The girl if she wants, but not the other one!"

"Girl?" Howard asked in confusion. "I don't know what you're going on about, Benny. Just hold your horses and I'll go get Bryson."

A moment or two passed as they waited in silence. A falling mist of sprinkling rainfall faintly pattered all around. It could be seen as a soft spray passing in front of the distant lamp light, and lay on their bodies as a delicate dew.

Footsteps on the other side of the wall finally approached, followed by the rustling of a latch. A door opened on the opposite side of a rectangular notch cut in the wall. Out of that hole appeared two faces, peering through at the party.

"Let's have a look at you then," Howard said, gesturing for them to step forward.

When the two men caught sight of Uriel, they responded with wide eyes and hushed conversation amongst themselves.

"This is my friend," Malala spoke up. "His name is Uriel. I've known him now for—"

"We'll have to ask Tay about this one," Bryson interrupted.

"You should ask my father about this!" Ben shouted from the dark.

"We'll be back shortly!" Howard called through the hole, ignoring Ben's remark.

With that, the two men closed the wooden hatch and latched it. Another longer moment passed. The rain started to grow. Louder and wetter. Fat drops splashed against the surrounding canopy and beat on the wood wall. It drenched their hair and flesh in a cold shower, making the long wait all that much longer. At least for the three men and women with flesh. Uriel stood in the shower as still as a statue, as rain ran down his metal skin.

Finally, on the other side of the wall, came the muffled shuffle of footsteps and hushed words between the pitter-patter of rainfall. The little wood door opened once more, and three faces now peered out. The newest of them, the crumpled, kindly visage of an old woman.

"Oh my!" the old woman exclaimed as her eyes widened. She followed up with a "Ha!" A nearly winking eye and an open, tilted smirk on her worn face betrayed a mixture of surprise and bemusement.

"What do you make of it, Mama Tay?" Howard asked.

"Some kind of—of… robot man!" With that, Mama Tay started to openly laugh. A reaction that only added to everyone's confusion.

"Greetings," Uriel stated with a modest wave. "My name is Uriel."

"Oh my… and he talks," Mama Tay remarked.

"I am capable of communicating in a number of human languages," Uriel responded.

"Well then…" Mama Tay stated, still marveling at the sight of the robot man on the other side of the wall. "I guess even robot men need to get out of the rain, don't they?" She then turned to the two men to her side. "Well, boys… You know quarantine dock protocol. Get to it."

"Uh, yes. Okay, very well then." Howard turned to Uriel and Malala. "Stand there a moment. We're gonna scan everyone through the wall."

Ben silently ground his teeth in the dark.

After a bit of shuffling, Howard's hand stretched through the hole in the wall. A hand holding some kind of curved device vaguely resembling a pistol with a spindly cable attached to its base.

Malala felt intimidated by this new development and instinctively stepped back. Uriel reached out and gently held her in place. "It appears to be a pathogen analyzer," he explained quietly. "The scan should be complete momentarily."

The hand then withdrew, and after a series of beeps, Howard spoke up. "Looks all good. You can escort them to the gate."

"Very good," Marco replied, and then turned to Malala and Uriel. "If you'll follow me, then."

Marco led the two through the large wooden doors as they slowly parted, while Ben trailed behind in the dark, muttering curses under his breath.

"Don't forget to lock it tight this time," Howard called to Bryson as they swung the doors closed.

"Yeah, yeah, I've got it," Bryson shot back, annoyed.

"Last time, you left the latch up and the doors were swinging wide open."

"Look, it's locked. Alright?"

The two men continued bickering in the night, as Marco, Malala, Uriel, and Ben trudged along. Once they all were through the gate, Ben marched off into the dark with only the barest wave goodbye. Marco nodded silently to Ben's gesture before watching with a sigh as his partner walked away.

Marco led the remaining party down the gradual, sloping main dirt street of the little "town." A smattering of log cabins, with a number of makeshift shelters in between. The log wall through which they had passed stretched out in the dark and boxed in the whole area, making it something of a large fort. But those connecting walls could not be seen at night. Dark shadows which blended into their inky surroundings amidst the cold, dark, rainy night.

"Here we are," Marco announced. "The guest lodge." He then opened the door with a long creak, before stepping inside and fiddling with something in the dark. After a moment, he brought forth a lit lantern and gestured for Uriel and Malala to enter. "After you…"

78

XIV

MARCO gave Uriel and Malala a tour of the little lodge and its amenities. An indoor fireplace stood in the center of the space, with a long flue ascending to the ceiling. Atop a small stairway of three or four steps rested a little alcove of a room, in which lay a neatly made bed. To the side was a small kitchen and dining room, with assorted cabinets above and below clean counters—counters which remained largely in good condition. Embedded within those counters rested a sink. A sink with a spout which gushed forth fresh water. Clean potable water, rushing out on demand. This miracle of indoor plumbing was especially wondrous to Malala, who slowly raised and lowered the handle at least half a dozen times, marveling each moment the crystal clear torrent would rush out like magic.

Half an hour passed, as Marco went on to tell Malala all about the town and its history. Camp Town it was called. Originally a camping resort of sorts in the before times. It had since been expanded over the years as folks from other areas—largely from mountain tops and other distant locales outside the cities and towns—came and settled alongside its original inhabitants. Mama Tay was one of the oldest residents, her parents having worked for the "forest service" before their untimely death.

Just as Marco was relating what he knew of Mama Tay's parents, a knock came at the door, quickly followed by the voice of Mama Tay herself. "Knock knock."

A smile could be heard in that voice, and Marco responded to it with a silent smile of his own as he rose to open the door. Firelight washed over a grinning, wrinkled face. An amber face filled with ripples and creases which looked all the more crumpled in the dim light, and a visage all the more bronze in that light's yellow hue. Bright white braided hair, matched by a white toothy grin.

"Am I interrupting anything?"

Marco turned to Malala and then back. "No, no, not at all."

Mama Tay's grin grew wider. "Well, that's too bad. Maybe next time." With that, she gave the young man a wink, and stepped inside, plopping along slowly with a small wooden staff she used as a kind of cane. He responded with an awkward chortle and a bit of a blush. Malala looked between the two and gave them both a puzzled expression.

"Greetings," Uriel said from his position further inside. His utterance was accompanied by his standard slow hand wave.

Mama Tay's grin faded slightly, and turned into a bit of a smirk as she narrowed her eyes in thought. She stared at Uriel this way for a small moment before slowly nodding her head. "Uriel, was it?"

"Indeed."

"I suppose I never introduced myself proper. My name is Teófila. But folks around here call me Mama Tay." She took a pause and looked around the room, nodding rhythmically as she leaned on her staff. Everyone else remained still and silent. Uriel retained his standard blank expression, while Malala and Marco looked on at the woman warmly with quiet respect. "You two can call me Tay too if you'd like. I've also been known to go by 'old lady,' 'granny,' and 'hey you.' In short, you can call me what you'd like… or call me what you don't like." Marco and Malala chuckled in amusement, before she continued. "But if you call me something *I* don't like, just don't be surprised if I pretend not to hear you. It's easier to do these days, since my hearing ain't as good as it used to be."

"My name is Malala," Malala stated nervously with a warm smile. A lingering symptom of the old woman's own infectious charm.

Mama Tay and Uriel exchanged nods, before Mama Tay turned to Uriel and spoke again. "I've never met a robot man before. I remember, as a little girl, seeing something like this— like *you…* Uriel. I thought it was all just fantasy. Fantasy for boys at that. But I guess the world then was filled with wonders I never knew…" She gazed off at some point beyond. Old weary eyes, pink and yellow in the corners, glazed over with the misty residue of a sea of memories.

After a moment, Mama Tay let out a sigh and returned to the present with a half-hearted smile. "I'm sure Marco has given you the grand tour."

Malala nodded and smiled.

"Good, good. If there's anything you need, child, don't hesitate to ask. We try to be very welcome around here. Well… *most* of us."

"Thank you, I will."

Mama Tay nodded warmly as she turned and looked at each of the three in silence for a moment, before letting out a peaceful sigh. "I suppose I should get on back to the dust bin. Pleasure to meet you both." She then turned to Marco and said, "Don't stay too long now, yeah? I'm sure our guests could use some rest."

Marco nodded with a smile. "I was just about to head out, myself. Can I escort you home?"

"I got here just fine. I'm sure I can get back just as well. I know how to steer clear of a puddle or two." The kindly aged woman cracked open the door as she spoke, and started to hobble outside.

"Alright, alright," Marco replied with a soft laugh. "Have a good night, Mama Tay."

"You too, Marco. I meant what I said. Give the girl a chance to sleep now."

"Yes, yes, of course."

With that, she turned and walked away, slowly plodding along with her staff in the dark. Marco watched her for a moment, before gently closing the door.

"Well, it's been a pleasure," he said. "I should get going, as promised."

"Thank you," Malala replied, "for everything."

Marco smiled and nodded. "Have a good night, Malala." He then turned to the metal man and nodded in polite acknowledgment. "Uriel."

Once Marco had gone, Malala turned to Uriel and asked, "What's a dust bin?"

XV

WHETHER due to the incredibly comfortable mattress or the long day filled with constant travel, Malala experienced the best night of sleep she could ever remember. The morning was late when she awoke. When she did, she discovered Uriel was gone.

In a mild panic and a fog of confusion, Malala quickly dressed and rushed out the door of the cabin to immediately find a crowd gathered outside.

"Perfect, yes!" a man exclaimed. A man that Malala could now see in a gap between the backs of spectators. He was standing next to Uriel, smiling. As she came closer, the crowd parted a little. "Here and here," the man stated as he made some quick markings on a large pipe. Uriel then grabbed the pipe with both hands at the points of the markings. Then, in a feat of strength and precision, he bent the pipe at a perfect 90-degree angle.

"Uriel?" Malala called out.

"Good morning," Uriel stated and gave his customary wave.

"What are you doing, Uriel?"

"I was just borrowing your robot here to help me with these new water pipes," the man interjected. "It's really handy with our hydraulic bender needing to be repaired and all."

Your robot. The words echoed in Malala's mind. And they didn't sit well in her heart. "Uriel is my friend," Malala stated somewhat sternly, her eyes narrowed and fixed on the man. "He can do as he pleases."

"Uh…" the man simply replied, sensing her quiet hostility as he quickly darted his eyes from her to Uriel and back.

"Is that what you wish to do?" Malala asked Uriel.

Uriel stood up straight and gave Malala a soft smile. "I am happy to be of service."

"Yes, well, I gotta say your, uh, your *friend…* he's really helpful, that's for sure."

Malala glanced between Uriel and the man, coldly assessing the scene before her in silence. Finally, she turned to Uriel. "You don't have to do anything you don't want, okay?"

"Of course," Uriel said with a quiet nod and that same subdued smile of his.

"Good morning!" a familiar voice called from behind. Malala turned to see the beaming face of Marco. He was standing a few yards away with a paper bag in his hand. "Have you had breakfast yet?"

Malala couldn't help but return that smile in kind. "No, actually. I, uh, just got up."

"Would you care to join me then?"

"Right now?"

"Sure, why not?"

Malala became acutely aware of how long she had gone without washing. Her hair was a mess and she likely smelled. Back home on the mountain, she tried to wash herself every other day. When the waterfall ran, she'd dance in its cascade. When it was dry, she'd use a wash cloth. Her father sometimes scoffed at her routine. He might go more than a month without so much as a rinse.

"You'll smell a lot better," she told him once.

"My nose works well enough," he had replied, smirked, and tapped his nostril.

Ever since living alone, and then with Uriel, her routine had lapsed. But that wasn't the only reason she blushed as she looked up into Marco's eyes.

"Can you—can you give me a little time? I'll just, uh, just a little…"

"Yes, of course," Marco said warmly with a nod.

◆

Once she had a moment to freshen up—the magical running shower in the lodge was a very useful marvel indeed—Malala tied her hair back and tried to make herself as presentable as possible. She only wished she had a change of clothes now. When she finished preparing, she invited Marco back in, and he revealed a small basket of fresh eggs, a couple potatoes, and an assortment of herbs. The yield of a small chicken coop, and the community garden on the edge of town, which had been steadily expanding for years now.

They dined and chatted for over an hour as the morning turned to noon. A pleasant bright noon with only the smallest hint of a cool breeze. A typical warm winter's day in the mountains of a land once called California.

As they finally emerged from the lodge, Malala noticed rows of paper bags along the stone walkway snaking its way through the small village of cabins that made up the town. "What are these for?" she asked.

"They're for tonight. Tomorrow is the start of Advent and all."

"Advent?"

"Yeah. Every year, we celebrate it. Lights and gifts and things."

"Why? What is it for?"

"It's uh… well… it's, heh, I don't know. Maybe you should ask Mama Tay. I think she probably told me once before, and I forgot."

◇

They toured the town together. Stonework trails snaking between old wood cabins and new cloth tents scattered here and there on the sloping ground of a gentle forest valley. He showed her the old ranger station cabin, a place of some historic significance which he had forgotten. The growing garden, where they grew potatoes and tomatoes and a number of other plants—the names of which he had mostly forgotten. And finally the town hall. An ancient wood lodge filled with metal folding chairs, with every wall lined with windows— more than a dozen in total. Immediately outside the front entrance was a quaint display. A peculiar collection of crumbling antique figurines huddled around the effigy of a baby in a bed of dead leaves. Malala was most significantly curious about this peculiar scene, but—again—it was something with which Marco was… less than familiar.

Malala gazed at the scene for some time in silence. She noted every detail. Father and mother. Infant child between them. Beasts of burden behind them. Simple, and yet strangely profound. It spoke something to her, but she could no more read its message than she could read text.

Marco finally broke the silence. "The mayor wants to meet you tonight."

"Mayor?"

"Well, you and Uriel both. It's been a while since our little town has had guests."

Malala nodded quietly, her eyes still fixed on the scene. Her mind wandered through it, and beyond. Her eyes lingering on the mother as she absently caressed her belly.

"Shall I say you'll both be there?"
"There…? Oh. I guess, yes. I will ask Uriel too."

Jonathan Lee

XVI

THE sun had long since passed beyond the forested hillside of Mount Wilson in the west. The last remains of a red twilight danced from distant clouds, as Uriel and Malala followed Marco to the door of a large cabin rising prominently on the northern slope of town. It was one of the town's newer constructions, and a large one—larger even than town hall.

They were all greeted by an attendant at the door. A kindly young woman with a warm smile who waved farewell to Marco before ushering Malala and Uriel inside. "This way, please," she said as she guided them from the foyer through a hallway, and into a large dining room.

At the head of the table was an older man with a nicely coiffed crew cut of silver hair resting above a worn face with ice blue eyes. His exceeding height was apparent as he rose from his seat and greeted his guests with a cold, formal smile. "Ah, just on time. Thank you both for joining me."

Malala nodded awkwardly and glanced about the room in quiet timidity and unspoken concern.

"Malala was it?" the man asked.

"Yes."

"And… Uriel, correct?"

"Indeed," Uriel replied and returned his standard warm smile.

"Please, have a seat. I'm so glad you both could join us tonight."

The "us" to which the man referred, and to whom he gestured, consisted of a gray-haired woman to his left, and a blond boy seated to his right. A young man with a barely constrained scowl beneath two strangely angular eyebrows. A face which Malala immediately recognized with equal measures of trepidation and irritation... Ben.

Noting Malala's reaction, the tall older man gestured to Ben. "I understand you met my son earlier, when he escorted you during one of his patrols."

Malala nodded and glanced at Ben briefly. Ben clenched his jaw and glared in return.

"My son has an abundance of... caution." With this last word, the older man glanced toward Uriel. "I apologize for any... misunderstanding."

Malala retained a blank expression as she glanced between Ben and his father for a lingering moment. Finally, she spoke. "*I* understand. I hope your son does now as well. Uriel is my friend."

"Oh yes, of course," the man replied. "Isn't that right, Ben?"

Ben, in turn, remained silent and simply nodded sheepishly. Malala stared coldly at the young man, as he averted his eyes and stared at the table.

The man coughed nervously, before continuing. "My name is Charles Bloodgood. I am the mayor of this fair town. This is my wife, Elizabeth. And of course... Ben."

Malala nodded and tried to give a polite smile to them all, before glancing about awkwardly. The tension in the room was then interrupted by a man in formal attire quietly setting a plate of food in front of the man at the head of the table.

"Ah, excellent," he remarked with a practiced smile. "What are we having tonight, Mr. Carter?"

"Cucumber salad with olives, Mr. Mayor, followed by our main course of braised venison with rosemary and shiitake. Our dessert tonight will be Crème Brûlée."

"Ah, very good. I'm glad to see our remote metro valley greenhouse finally being put to good use." The mayor then turned to Malala. "Just out of an abundance of consideration, I had courses prepared for… your friend. Although, am I right in assuming—?"

"Uriel does not eat."

"I had thought as much, yes. Uriel, is there anything we might otherwise get for you…? Oil perhaps?" This last question was accompanied by a teasing smirk.

"My internal nanoprocessing center is capable of synthesizing any lubricant as needed."

"Ah, very well. I jest, of course."

Uriel returned a quiet blank smile. Malala in turn looked to him to assess his response before turning back to the mayor and giving a polite smirk. She then prodded at an olive on her plate with her fork before carefully testing its taste in her mouth. A curiously sharp and salty flavor she'd never experienced before. After chewing it over a bit, she decided it was suitably edible and finally swallowed. One of a number of things she would carefully chew over before the night was done…

◇

They dined and conversed for the better part of an hour. The mayor was an aloof but perfectly cordial man. After sharing a bit about the town and its history—much of which Malala had already learned from Marco earlier—he went on to asking Uriel about his own background and history.

91

Through this exchange, Malala learned a number of things about Uriel she had never known before. Things she had never thought to ask—or understood enough to do so.

For one, the mayor actually recognized the name of the "Institute" from which Uriel hailed and had some vague secondhand recollection of its scope and purpose. Uriel explained how he actually remembered being in stasis. His consciousness had arisen within a simulated environment in which he and other virtual entities engaged in an assorted number of assessments and iterative processes, the nature of which was difficult to put into words precisely. Malala was subsequently surprised to learn that this mode of existence went on for years. Of course, as Uriel conceded, the exact length of the experience was difficult to assess objectively, and his experience of the passage of time may have been altered since finally awakening.

When he did so, he had found himself in the empty remains of a lab connected to a massive data center powered by a private, secure power station built to operate autonomously and indefinitely. In his experience within the simulation, he had had access to an enormous library of assorted media. A kind of archive of all the world's knowledge bundled together in a giant representative snapshot of the fabled Internet—that great achievement of human civilization from the end of the 20th century, which had since gone dark with the progressive failures of the power grid and other infrastructure that came with the "great fading."

The "great fading" was how the mayor referred to the great disaster that befell the world with the advent of SOS. This term was perhaps a bit of a misnomer, as it was initially accompanied by panic, rioting, martial law, and all manner of terror and upheaval. But that didn't last very long in the end. The disease spread, and most of the world's population grew old before its time. Isolated pockets remained in remote regions. Disconnected homesteads, camps, and communes. The invisible chatter of encoded transmissions disappeared from the air. The buzzing rumble of traffic slowed and then stopped. Stars returned to the night skies of silent cities. In the end, the world had indeed... faded away.

Through the course of this conversation, the mayor's wife remained mostly quiet, politely interjecting on occasion to make some light remark on local matters pertaining to the town and its communal efforts. All the while, Ben ate his food in silence, appearing to listen on occasion but mostly staying seated only begrudgingly. His default expression was a mixture of listlessness and irritation.

Ben's expression changed, however, in the midst of one of his father's monologues. "We have actually had great success in our agricultural endeavors," his father had been saying. "As I mentioned before, our crop production goes quite well beyond what you see simply around the perimeter of our little town. We have greater yields of many varieties in a scattered remnant of land plots, miles away. It is more than enough to sustain our community—more than enough indeed to accommodate tremendous growth, in fact. It's simply unfortunate about this entire... Alejandro situation."

The mayor had sighed with this last statement, and at the mention of the name "Alejandro," Ben's ears perked up. His expression changed from one of abject boredom to one of concern—if not outright fear.

Malala noted the change. The dread that seemed to fall over the room at the mention of the name. She glanced between Uriel and the mayor before breaking the silence. "What is Alejandro?"

"Hmph," the mayor noted. A soft sad laugh escaping through the nostrils of a somber face. "You pose a better question than you may realize. For some may say the answer is 'a man.' But there is good reason to doubt that assumption..."

"Huh?"

"Alejandro styles himself the 'Governor of California,' heh. But his claim is just as mythical as the land he claims to govern. In truth, Alejandro is a warlord. A brutal tyrant who holes himself up in a stronghold many miles to the north."

"Oh… what is the… *situation*, then?"

"Every season he demands a 'tax.'"

As his father spoke these words, Ben gritted his teeth and shook his head with greater irritation than he had shown yet. He then spoke up, himself. "It's not fair."

"Indeed," his father said and shook his head in agreement. "He sends his goons on horseback to intimidate us, and make his demands known."

"We shouldn't have to give up our resources for… *outsiders*." With this last word, Ben stared at Uriel.

"We do what we must, Ben."

Glancing between the mayor and his son, Malala then spoke up. "Thank you… for the meal. You have made us both very welcome."

The mayor nodded and gave a quiet smile. "Hospitality is a virtue. Thereby some have entertained angels."

"Angels?" Malala asked.

"It's an old quote, as I recall," the mayor explained. "Our fair town has had numerous guests over the years. Some have stayed and some have gone. Some have been a burden, but many have been a blessing."

At that, Ben spoke up again. "It's not always obvious which is which or what others might be capable of…"

"Indeed," the mayor said. "It's not always clear what… *hidden talents*… others may have to offer our community."

Malala looked on as his father stared at Ben for a brief pause, while the son averted his eyes and gritted his teeth. "Yes, well… thank you again. I think we should get going."

"Certainly," the mayor said. "You are more than welcome…"

XVII

WHEN Malala opened the door to her cabin, she discovered Marco and Mama Tay already inside. They were seated across from each other, both with old playing cards in their hands.

"Go fish," Mama Tay said to Marco, her failing ears failing to hear the door. He turned and gestured to Malala. She, in turn, turned to the door and let out a wide grin. "There you are, child. How was your dinner with ol' Chucky?"

"Chucky?" Malala replied.

Marco chuckled quietly and shook his head.

"The mayor," Mama Tay explained as she gestured for Malala to sit. "I've known Chuck—sorry, Charles—since he was smaller than you, child. He was little Chucky then. Just barely walking when the Bloodgoods joined the camp. I was only a little girl myself, but I still had to look out for little Chucky like everybody else. Times have a way of changin'…"

The old woman and Marco exchanged smiles before Marco turned to Malala. "Would you like me to deal you in?"

"I'm not sure I know how to play."

"We can teach you," Marco replied. "Give a man a fish, he eats for a day, but—"

"Give a mother a fish," Mama Tay interjected with a twinkle in her eye, "and she'll eat for two."

Malala smiled and caressed the swell of her own fleshy hatchery, quietly teeming with life in the water of her womb.

◇

The four played cards late into the night. Mama Tay regaled everyone with tales of the town's past. Marco shared several amusing anecdotes of his time spent as a ranger—including one involving Ben getting chased by a deer. They had switched from "Go Fish" to "War" and then "Gin Rummy" before finally settling on "Poker." This one they came to last, as Mama Tay had half-jokingly expressed concerns about Uriel having "the most uncanny poker face I have ever seen."

Finally, after a moment of silence followed a little bout of laughter, Malala looked to Mama Tay and asked, "What is Advent?"

"I told her you'd know best," Marco interjected.

"Ah, Advent, you say?" Mama Tay asked.

Malala replied with a nod. "The lights and things."

"Ah, yes. Well… It gets cold this time of year. Not as cold as in other parts of the world. Well, at least that's what I always was told. Can't say I've traveled much. I have the oldest, foggiest kind of memory of riding in an airplane once. At least, I think that's what it was. I think my momma told me that's what it was. It was loud and fast and exciting. Hearing some kind of loud rumble outside. Getting pulled back in my seat. Seeing the ground fall away out this little window…"

"You were saying it gets cold?" Malala asked, coaxing her back to the topic at hand, after Mama Tay drifted off into a sea of nostalgia. Malala had learned the necessity of doing this from time to time at this point.

"Yes, right. Well, then, it's nice to get together this time of year. When the nights are cold and long. Kind of like we're doing. And we also give gifts to one another. It helps us remember to be grateful for everything we've got—even when it sometimes doesn't seem like a lot."

"Why is it called 'Advent?'"

"Well now that's probably a good question for Rasheed. He fancies himself a historian and all. And he does certainly seem to read a lot."

"Rasheed…" Malala half-whispered, saying the name aloud as a mental note.

"In the meantime, all I really can tell you is that it has something to do with the Baby Jesus."

"The baby in the cradle?"

"Yes. It was always called a 'manger' for some reason. The old good book tells about how that baby grew up to do a lot of extraordinary things. Walking on water and feeding folks. Savior of the world."

"Savior of the world?"

Mama Tay grew somber and nodded her head. "I guess the world got lost again." She let out a sigh and forced a smile. "But nothing lasts forever, does it? Anyhow, all those stories from what went before aside, it's a nice time of year… for a *not*-so-nice time of the year. Seems like it's always best to try to make the best of things. And that, at least, makes sense to me."

Malala caressed her belly as she thought of her own baby. After a moment of quiet contemplation, she looked to Mama Tay again. "This last summer… did one night anyone see… falling fire? Many streaks across the sky at night."

"Falling fire?" Mama Tay asked, furrowing her brow.

"I remember," Marco interjected. "The shooting stars. And those two or three blazing fiery streaks. A truly brilliant display."

"Ah, yes, yes, of course," Mama Tay said. "What was it Rasheed had said?"

"He explained it was most likely those 'satellites' finally falling."

"Satellites?" Malala asked.

"From the world before," Mama Tay explained. "High up in the sky above the clouds. Men used to throw rockets into the sky, so fast and so far that they never would fall. Just keep flying around and around. At least that's what I understood. But then, there again… nothing lasts forever, does it?"

"No," Malala replied, "I guess not…"

XVIII

IN 1934, one year into FDR's "New Deal," construction completed on the Cogswell dam. But this reservoir project was not actually part of any of FDR's efforts. Its construction began two years prior in 1932, and funding for the project had been secured years before the Great Depression—bonds having been issued in 1924.

It wasn't nearly as sturdy as the Hoover Dam, a power station that had long fallen into disrepair, whose walls would nevertheless stand for ten thousand years. Like many smaller dams throughout the country once known as the United States, Cogswell was originally built to only last a century or less.

The dam had been renovated several times. Its sediment bed had been replaced after wildfires that swept across the land at the beginning of the 21st century, and its concrete wall slab had been patched on multiple occasions. Like everything else in the world, it became neglected subsequent to the "great fading." Subtle cracks had started to form in the dam's concrete face, and one day water would seep its way through the once impermeable membrane of the dam and slip between the mass of rocks making up the bulk of its body. When that happened, the dam would quickly collapse.

But that was all yet future. For now, as Marco and Malala stood atop the walkway at the crest of the concrete wall, they were faced with simple peace and tranquility. Sunlight danced on the glittering surface of the crystal reservoir, as tiny waves rippled in a gentle passing breeze.

"Beautiful…" Malala half-whispered the word in quiet awe. Never in her life had she stood so close to such a vast body of water.

"It is, isn't it?" Marco asked with a smile. "Was it worth the hike?"

Malala nodded quietly as she took in the sight.

"I'm seriously impressed we went as quickly as we did… considering." With this last word, Marco gazed down at her burgeoning belly. It had been two weeks since they met, and her abdomen had notably swelled within that time.

"Heh," she snorted, "I may be with child, but I am not…" She paused, searching for the word. One of the words she had picked up from Uriel. What was it again? "I am not an… *invalid.*"

"Of course," Marco replied with a warm nod. "You are one of the most capable women I've met."

"Well…" she replied, and blushed. "You're pretty capable yourself… for a man."

They both exchanged a chortle or two, before Marco caught his breath. And then, gazing into her auburn eyes, he spoke now warmly but very seriously. "Malala… I—I've only known you for a short time now. But… I feel we may have something. Something, together. If you would have me at—at your side… I would be honored."

She found herself surprised, although in retrospect she felt she shouldn't have. Perhaps it was simply a matter of her habit of tempering expectations. She had faced enough tragedy and hardship to keep such a disposition. And so the thought that Marco might actually like her as much as she liked him was something she had only entertained as a quiet fantasy.

Malala loved the kindness in his eyes. She admired that about him most of all. A strong man with a soft heart. And as she gazed now in those eyes, he started to speak again.

"If you would have me, I could raise your child as my own. I have—"

She interrupted him with a kiss. A gentle peck on the corner of his lips. Certainly not on the cheek, but not perfectly centered either. A deliberate gesture of tentative affirmation. And then as she drew back, she smiled, nodded, and simply uttered "Yes."

Marco quickly grew a wide grin, before embracing her. They rocked back and forth and gazed out at the reservoir together in quiet glee. No more words were needed for now, and they both enjoyed the silence in peace.

Jonathan Lee

XIX

S EVERAL months passed. The days grew warmer, the nights grew shorter, and winter turned to spring. Uriel continued to be a great asset to the town—entirely by his choice, as Malala was quick to remind everyone. Not everyone was quick to make use of his help. And some even resented it for one reason or another—none of which were entirely rational reasons. Malala, herself, tried to be an asset to her new community, but that grew increasingly difficult as her feet swelled and her back ached as her pregnancy progressed.

Then, one day, it happened. In the late morning of a cool spring day, Malala's water broke. Mama Tay had her ushered to her own cabin, where she was attended by two women in town who had some experience with midwifery. Over the course of several hours, they had her bathe, accompanied her on some light walks around town, and generally accommodated her needs as her contractions became increasingly frequent and more uncomfortable.

It was twilight by the time she started to deliver. And after half an hour of toil, suffering, and a few roars of pain, the tiny newborn arrived. The warm cabin was filled with the loud squeaky wails of the little child, announcing his own arrival with his cry—much to the laughing relief of all, Malala included.

Soaked in sweat, Malala looked down at the tiny creature in her arms, its bare flesh against her own, and smiled. "I will name him Ander." Then, looking to the midwives in attendance, she explained, "It was my father's name."

They encouraged her to nurse her newborn, and so she did. Fortunately, her milk had come in weeks prior. Ander latched on well and started to immediately suckle.

"Little Ander," Mama Tay said with a smile, as she reached out to stroke the tiny boy's delicate head. Malala looked to the old woman with a mixture of exhausted relief and gratitude.

After a moment, the old woman exclaimed a little "Oh" as she suddenly remembered something. "I almost forgot. Rasheed asked me to give this to you."

"What is it?"

"He calls it a 'holorecorder.' He said something about 'lie dar' and 'projector arrays' and… I didn't understand it all. But maybe Uriel can help you work the thing. We only have two in town. Rasheed thought you could record your baby. Something to help you remember Ander when you both get older."

"Thank you," Malala said, as she turned over the cubic bulky contraption in her hand, and looked it over with some puzzlement.

"Enjoy it while it lasts. They grow up so fast."

Malala simply nodded, as she set down the device.

Mama Tay stayed for a while, adoring the little infant, before finally turning to Malala again. "I should be getting back to things. You take care, now, child."

"Thank you… for everything."

"You are always more than welcome," Mama Tay replied, with a warm smile, before she hobbled her way out of the cabin.

A moment or two passed before a knock came at the door, and slowly a cautious bronze face peaked inside.

"Marco!" Malala called with a hoarse voice. "Come in, come in..."

He stepped forward with some trepidation, a wide brim hat in both hands, kept in front of him. With a cautious smile, he glanced about the room and gently marched toward the bed where Malala was nursing.

"Wow..." he whispered. The faintest breath of a whisper as he stood in awe at the side of her bed. Malala looked to him, but his eyes were fixed on the little creature at her breast. Golden wisps of hair and soft sealed eyes emerging just above layers of fabric. A tiny rhythmic suckling sound echoed in the reverent silence. "Your child..." he said, in an astonished, hushed tone. "He's so... *beautiful.*"

They both remained in a serene silence for a plentiful moment of peace. Finally, after a sigh and a long groan, Malala half whispered to the nearest midwife, "Would it be okay if I stretched my legs?"

"If you feel like it. Just take it slow and easy..."

"I will."

XX

WITH slow, creaking steps, Malala ambled across the floor with Marco at her side. She took one lingering look at Ander and gave a weak, tired smile. He was fast asleep now in a bedside bassinet.

As the two exited the cabin, Uriel was there waiting outside.

"Greetings," Uriel said in his usual calm, even tone.

"Uriel," Malala replied with a pure wide grin, pulling her tired eyes almost closed.

One of the midwives came outside then to check on her. A young woman named Christina who had become Malala's friend over several months stood nearby and gave a little wave. Malala acknowledged everyone's presence with a wave of her own, accompanied by a weak smile.

"I thought it would be prudent to examine you and your child to assess your condition. May I proceed?"

"Yes, of course."

As soon as she nodded, Uriel's eyes rolled back in their sockets, and the usual blue light turned to red. The scanning plane washed over her body up and down, before turning off. He then stepped into the cabin and walked forward and began scanning the child as well.

Murmurs and hushed gasps within and without the cabin chattered in the air. Rushed footsteps stomped away from the cabin. The chattering grew. As Uriel exited the cabin, a small crowd was gathering.

"There!" a man exclaimed, as he ran up to the cabin with a younger man by his side. "I saw it with my own eyes!"

The younger man approached swiftly with a scowl. A young man who looked angry, afraid, disgusted, and delighted all at once. A man who looked as though he had been waiting for this moment for some time. The mayor's son nearly spit when he spoke out in a raised voice, "I knew this day would come! You're coming with me now, metal man!"

"Ben," Marco scoffed. "What is this all about?"

"I have a witness here. He told me—with no small alarm —that *Uriel* here shot some kind of fire light from his eyes."

"Ben, you're overreacting. I'm sure—"

Just then, Bryson interrupted. He had been frantically running, and by the time he approached Marco and Ben, he was shouting in a huff. "Marco! Benjamin! You're needed, sirs! At the gate! Alejandro! His men are here!"

Ben grew concerned for a moment, furrowing his brow. But he could not be deterred now. "Bryson, take Marco to the gate, and then inform my father at once. I am attending to other matters."

"Ben, we should go to the gate. You're wasting—"

"I am taking Uriel to the old station for questioning. This is *not* going to wait."

Marco gritted his teeth, as Uriel glanced between the two of them. He then spoke up. "I will submit to this inquiry."

Malala then spoke up. "What is this all about, Ben? Uriel was only helping me and my baby."

"Stay out of this, woman," Ben replied in scorn.

"Uriel is my friend. *Our* friend. You're being ridiculous!"

"He's already agreed," Ben stated coldly. "What was it you always say? *Uriel can do what he wants…*"

Malala gritted her teeth and scowled.

Marco then shook his head and sighed, before turning to Bryson. "Let's go."

"Wait!" Malala called out. She looked between the two groups as Ben gestured to Uriel. Whatever Ben had in mind for Uriel, she knew he could take care of himself. But as she looked off at the gate in the distance, a disquieting shadow fell on her heart. "I'm coming with you."

"You need rest," Marco pleaded.

"I'm coming with you," she stated again and gave him an unrelenting stare.

"Fine," he said with a sigh. "Just keep your distance and stay safe."

◇

"It's standard procedure now," Howard was saying when Marco and Malala arrived. Mama Tay was already standing nearby as Howard fumbled with the quarantine scanner.

"Do what you will, old man," a voice called through the gate. A cruel raspy voice that gave Malala chills as the sound crawled through the wall.

"Here, here," Bryson half whispered as he ran to Howard's side. He grabbed the scanner from him and operated its controls deftly, pointing the apparatus at the glaring eyes on the other side of the hole notched in the wall.

An aching long moment passed, and another man on the other side of the wall called out impatiently, "What's taking so long?"

"I've never seen this before," Bryson said to Howard.

"Are you sure you're doing it right?" Howard replied.

Mama Tay hobbled up to the men with her cane and steadied herself as she looked down at the device.

"What do you make of it, Mama Tay?"

"Hmm…" she uttered and scratched her head with her free hand. She rubbed her eyes. They didn't work as well as they used to. She wasn't sure if they could be trusted.

"Oh!" Bryson suddenly exclaimed. For a moment, Howard and Tay thought perhaps Bryson had stumbled upon some great insight into the matter. But instead, he continued, "I forgot to inform the mayor. I'll be right back!"

Bryson ran off, leaving old Howard and Tay scratching their heads over the strange unprecedented reading on the device. Meanwhile, Marco and Malala stood to the side, waiting anxiously.

"Your tax is due now! These delays are becoming insufferable! We will *not* leave empty-handed!"

Their calls went unanswered. The two elders ignored them as they instead whispered to each other, while peering over the apparatus.

The setting sun left crimson rays in the western half of a darkening sky, as Bryson finally returned, the mayor marching behind him. Tay and Howard slowly hobbled up to the mayor and showed them the strange readings on the quarantine scanner.

"Open the gate, now!" a man called out.

"In due time, gentlemen!" the mayor called out. "We have certain procedures we must follow here. It is for everyone's benefit. You must exercise some patience. We will honor our governor in good time."

"Enough!" one of the men shouted before banging on the gate in frustration.

Silence fell on both sides of the wall with that bang. Not on account of the loud clamorous thud that came from the man whacking his club against the wood, but instead, because of the slow, ominous creak that followed it. Bryson's forgetfulness had been the tool of fate. And in this moment, the men on the other side of the gate seized the opportunity which had presented itself. In a flash, that creaking crack of the open gate became a wide gaping portal, as the doors were flung open and the two men on horseback flooded through.

Everyone stepped back in shock as the two grizzled thugs rode through on their tall black beasts. They were pleased with their good fortune. An opportunity to show they meant business. A chance to intimidate the poor townsfolk and demonstrate they would use force if need be.

The mayor raised his hands, showing his palms in a gesture of pleading and a call for calm. He kept his voice steady as he slowly stepped back. "Now then, gentlemen…"

This confrontation may have gone like others in the past. They normally would have permitted the men inside. Normally, there wouldn't have been the strange readings, and they would have been cleared to enter anyway. The well-worn tradition had become a mere formality. The utility of which had been nearly forgotten.

But fate had something else in store that night.

As the two horsemen stood menacingly in the dark, one compelling his horse to rear upon its hind legs as a show of intimidation before cackling in delight, a voice called out from the distance.

A familiar young voice shouted into the dark, "Intruders!"

His shout was accompanied by a whistling whisper, followed quickly by a sharp thud. And then, shortly thereafter, a cry of pain. Ben had been waiting for some time to try out something new he had obtained and been training with of late. A bow and arrow set. His marksmanship was less than ideal. For, while he had been aiming for the man, center mass, he managed to just barely sink the arrow into the very corner of the man's shoulder.

"Gragh!" the man growled. He then drew an old rusted sword from a wood scabbard and in panic and sheer berserker rage, he lashed out at the nearest person he could find. That happened to be Marco, who was standing at the ready, spear in hand. The crazed thug knocked the spear out of Marco's hands with his crude sword, and swung again. In one grizzly swoop, he slashed through Marco's neck, before raising his sword up high and growling again at the top of his lungs.

"No!" Malala cried, as Marco fell to the ground, holding his neck desperately. Blood rushed through his fingers and down his chest, as he gurgled in shock and disbelief. Malala rushed to him, but there was nothing to be done.

At that same time, the thug's companion took this new development as a cue. And so he turned and reared up his horse in wrath and swung his club in fury. His club smashed its way into Mama Tay's abdomen, crushing her ribs and tearing her organs as she was lifted several feet off the ground. She tumbled to the ground, breaking several more bones on the way down.

The thugs kept swinging wildly, one knocking Howard's oil lamp out of his hands and tossing it yards away to a nearby wood cabin. When his companion caught sight of the fire, he looked to his own lamp and without another thought tossed it on the roof of another cabin.

"You will all pay for your treason!" the uninjured one called out, as his wounded companion winced and ground his teeth.

"Please!" the mayor pleaded. "We will comply with your demands! There is no more need for such violence!"

The injured thug, the arrow still lodged in his shoulder, scowled at the mayor before slowly dismounting and started to march up to the mayor in growing fury.

Malala's heart raced as she watched the scene unfold. In fear and desperation, she finally thought to call out to the one person who might make a difference in this whole growing disaster. "Uriel!" She called at the top of her voice. "Uriel, help! Please!"

He probably would have heard her voice had she whispered. As it was, he heard the commotion and had conjectured, even as the guards standing watch over him at the station listened in concern and confusion, but he was waiting patiently while continuing to comply with his detainment. All that changed when she called out.

He rushed past the guards, knocking them aside as peacefully as he could, as they fell aside offering as much resistance as dandelions in a hurricane. He ran up the town's main street like lightning, passing by Ben and Malala both in a flash.

The thug, with an expression of unabated malice and ferocity, swung his rusted sword down past the mayor's silver-haired head with every intent to slit the man's throat. As it came down, the sword clanged. His hand stopped short by half a foot in the air.

In confusion, the thug turned to see Uriel standing at his side, holding the man's sword by the blade in Uriel's outstretched hand.

"Gah! What the fuck is that?!" He backed away in sheer terror at the sight of the metal monster, his blade sliding out of Uriel's metal hand with a clinking hiss.

"I would advise you to leave this town immediately." Fully aware of its affect at this point, Uriel began a scan of the man and his companion, heightening their terror. And thus, with great haste, the one thug ran back to his horse and both scattered into the night.

The streets ran with blood. Marco's blood. The light in his eyes was gone. There was nothing more to be done for him, aside from affording him the honor in death that he had earned in life. But that would have to come later. For now, fires were blazing. The townsfolk were rushing in panic. And Mama Tay was writhing on the ground.

Uriel came to her at once, and Malala followed. He washed her in that same red light that had caused such alarm before. But she wasn't bothered in the slightest. Even if she hadn't been so distracted by her grave condition, it wouldn't have bothered her. She had always expected some surprises from the "robot man." All the more once she had become his friend.

"You are bleeding internally," Uriel stated upon completing his scan. "I may be able to halt the hemorrhaging if I begin emergency surg—"

"No," Mama Tay interrupted, between labored breaths. "It's coming now... I can feel it. You need... to help. The fires. Please... save our town."

Malala then spoke up. "Mama Tay, Uriel can help you! If there's anyone who—"

"No, child. Not much time. Others... hurt. Besides... I've lived long enough."

"No, please! Mama Tay, you... you have to..." Malala's voice cracked as an unhinged wheel of desperation rolled up her throat. She covered her mouth and trembled with a mixture of shock and despair. Like a sea swell, waves of pain and sadness rolled over her body, flooding her eyes with tears, and she began to sob. She fought away her feelings enough to speak, and with a twinge of anger amidst the sadness, she shouted out "Please, Mama, don't go!"

Whether she knew it or not, a part of Malala's heart was crying out to the mother she had never known. And now the mother she had just gotten to know was passing before her eyes. Mama Tay could sense this. She could hear it in Malala's voice. And so she gave the girl a soft smile of pity and stroked her hair.

"Uriel…" the old woman whispered, her eyes closed now.

"Yes?" Uriel responded, while coming closer.

"You should—you should go. But… before you do… I have been meaning to ask you something. Something for… some time."

"Please proceed."

"Everyone knows me as Tay."

"Mama Tay," Malala interjected, and squeezed the old woman's hand tightly with one hand, while wiping away tears with the other.

"Yes, that's right. Mama Tay. But Tay isn't really short for… for Teófila. It's for something else. They used to tell me something. Something with such… affection. It was in Español, but I always remember the words. Even if I have long… forgotten what they mean. Do you think… do you think you could tell me… what they mean?"

"I am fluent in a number of human languages," Uriel replied, "including Spanish."

"Yes, very good. They would tell me all the time. My mother… and father, too. And their eyes… as they said… it… I…"

With that, she started to drift off. Malala squeezed her hand harder. "Mama Tay?" she asked and gulped.

"Yes… yes. They would look at me and say… Tay-ahmo Meeha. What… Uriel… what does it… mean?"

"I believe the expression to which you—"

"What? Hard… to hear. Come closer…"

And so, Uriel lowered himself next to the old woman's ear and uttered a few words in a low voice. The old woman responded with a wide smile as tears streamed out from her closed eyes and down her wrinkled cheeks, running like little quiet creeks along the crevices of her weary countenance.

"Yes, of course" she half-whispered, before breathing out one long relaxed sigh. A final exhalation as she passed away in peace.

"Mama Tay?" Malala asked with a rising panic. "Mama Tay?!"

Uriel quickly scanned the old woman's frail form with his panning eyes, and gripped her wrist purposefully. After a moment, he turned to Malala and spoke, "She has expired."

Malala covered her face and sobbed. Uriel watched her quietly and waited. A soft wind blew. A gentle sound between impassioned shouts and scurry, as others scrambled to put out fires in the distance.

Finally, Malala spoke up, while sniffing and wiping away tears. "What did... what did it mean? Those words?"

"She appeared to say '*Te amo, mija*,' which is Spanish for... 'I love you, child.'"

With that, Malala turned back to the old woman and gazed at her kind, noble face. She stroked her hair, and kissed her forehead, anointing it with her tears. Mama Tay had been loved as much as a child, as she had been as a mother.

A wail rose up from behind. Malala's own child was crying. She turned back, gazing to the nearby cabin where her boy was. She had a duty to attend to, and Uriel had his. "Help with the fires," she commanded in an even voice, stoically.

With that, she rose up and walked away. There would be more than enough time to bury the dead. Now, she must attend to the living. And one new life in particular.

"Malala," a voice behind her called out. When she turned back, it was Ben. "Uriel... Malala, I'm... I'm so sorry."

She stared for a long moment into his eyes. The eyes of a boy in shock, terror, and confusion. She gazed into those eyes, searching and judging whether it was only that, or if there was any semblance of genuine remorse. In the end, she realized it was irrelevant.

And so, without another word, she turned and kept walking.

Jonathan Lee

XXI

"MALALA," Uriel stated, calling for her attention as he entered the lodge. She had just picked up little Ander and was rocking him in her arms to quell his crying.

"Yes?"

"You must leave town immediately."

A chill went down her spine and her eyes widened. And she uttered the first thing that came to her mind. "What? Why?" She gulped in confusion and fear. His simple statement had thrown her into as much turmoil as the tumult outside. And the fire that burned her from within grew from the one simple fact which she knew more intimately than most anything else: Uriel was serious. He was always serious. And she always trusted his insights. If she had to leave, it must be true. But where would she go now? Who could go with her? Physically exhausted, mentally distressed, struggling to keep herself together in the whirlwind of grief and fear with a crying newborn in her arms…

"My earlier scan revealed you have contracted SOS."

"Es oh… the disease? The aging…?" Her mind flashed back to the skeleton on the roadside.

"It is imperative you do not infect the others."

"Infect…" She looked down to Ander. At that moment, the greatest terror seized her mind and body. A dread that boiled up from her heart and filled every nerve. Her limbs started to quake, but she fought it. She had to hold on to her baby. But how much longer could she? How much longer would he…? "No, not Ander, no…"

"I have some curious news regarding your child. I want to perform another scan to be sure."

"Curious news?" She asked with a barely constrained, growing fury. She had always respected Uriel's cool calm. But now she struggled not to resent it.

"Please, it would be best for the community at large if we retreat immediately."

◇

Uriel quietly escorted Malala to the town's rear wall. Shouts and barking orders of every kind echoed throughout the little town, accompanied by the roar and crackle of distant flames. Away from that chaos, the mother and newborn retreated quietly in the dark, following Uriel's swift, purposeful steps.

"Where are we going? There's no gate here!" she exclaimed in a hushed tone, trying not to rouse the now sleeping child.

"Stand back, please." With that, Uriel grabbed one of the great logs of the town's wall and casually pulled it out of the ground, before gently setting it down with a quiet thud. "This way."

"Wait!" Malala exclaimed, in that same hushed tone, as they exited through the narrow opening in the wall. "What was the 'curious news?' Tell me about Ander!"

"Very well. This should be an effective proximity for the time being. One moment and I will begin the scan."

Malala waited with as much patience as she could muster, as that red plane of light passed over her child. And then again, the light passed over Malala and back to the child. Uriel delicately pressed one of his cold metal fingertips to the little boy's neck. The newborn barely stirred in response. And Malala was growing increasingly irritated.

"Well?" she asked, in between grinding her teeth.

"I have confirmed my initial analysis. Ander is immune."

"Immune?"

"Possibly the first of his kind. Thoroughly immune from the disease. I have suspected that there may be some individuals left who remain as passive carriers, but your child is a completely incompatible recipient. I suspect this may have something to do with his... *peculiar*... genetic background."

"So, you're saying... little Ander... he—he's... okay?"

"Indeed."

Malala let out a sigh. Her boy was okay. But then the shock and dread returned as she remembered her own condition. She was going to die? What then?

"Are you—are you sure? About me? I'm... I'm going to die?"

"That would appear to be an accurate prognosis, yes."

"If you're sure," she said with a gulp, "what about Ander? Are you sure he's going to be okay? Should he... should he stay?" Her head was whirling now. Instinctively, she lowered herself to the ground and rested little Ander in her lap. The weight of the world was crashing down on her shoulders, and she didn't know how much longer she could bear it. She had been so strong for so long. Death felt almost welcome compared to this perpetual burden. Pain, loss, turmoil, sadness, and confusion. Insecurity and doubt.

"There may still be time. Your child presents a unique opportunity."

"What do you mean?"

"Back at the Institute, I have access to lab equipment. With said equipment, it is entirely possible that I may be able to synthesize an effective treatment for your condition. Depending upon the outcome of my analysis, this may even take the form of a total mitigation."

"Okay, alright," Malala said, darting her eyes to and fro. "So we would go back to the Institute?"

"Indeed. I wish to scan the others in town for infection first."

"How long will that take?"

"I estimate approximately thirteen minutes."

"Okay… okay. I guess I—I'll see you soon…"

◇

Uriel was hardly noticed as the town's inhabitants ran to and fro, connecting and disconnecting hoses while raining down what water they could on the flames. All through this commotion, Uriel casually marched along, quietly washing everyone he could see in red light.

Meanwhile, Malala waited. The seconds ticked by like minutes. The minutes like hours. Alone. Utterly alone in the cold dark of night. The child in her arms was asleep now. The fires were dying down. Everything outside of her was turning to a state of quiet peace. But inside was a different story. The fires of pain, sadness, and anger were only growing. And still she waited.

She slowly rose to her feet when she saw Uriel approaching, carrying a large backpack and some kind of strap assembly in his right hand.

"I apologize for the three-minute delay. The scan was quicker than my initial estimate, but procuring supplies required more time." He then gestured to the large backpack strapped to his shoulders. Its base stretched below his waist, while its top exceeded his neckline. "I managed to acquire this 100-liter backpack from the ranger station. I have filled it with food and assorted items." He then extended the strap assembly in his hand to Malala. "This infant carrier is for you. It should be sufficient for newborns."

Malala nodded solemnly as she took the assembly in one hand and looked it over. "How is everyone else?"

"The remains of Mama Tay and Marco are infected. All remaining living entities in town are clear. Given the transmission vectors, the risk of subsequent infection is low, assuming everyone takes the routine precautions exercised with corpses."

"So I'm the only one…"

"That would appear to be the case, yes. We must leave immediately."

Malala slowly rose to her feet and gazed out toward town. Smoke rose from the dying embers of the last fires. Shadows wafting in a dark night. Black clouds seen in dark relief against a growing field of stars. There was nothing left for her in Camp Town now.

"Alright," she said, as cold as the night and as detached as the rolling clouds of smoke. "Let's go."

Jonathan Lee

XXII

THEY slowly marched up that same mountain trail they had taken months prior when they first came to Camp Town. The night wasn't as cold now as it was then, but having left in haste, Malala also wasn't as bundled up. Two hours passed in relative silence, as they slowly ascended. Uriel insisted Malala pace herself and stop occasionally to drink. Fortunately, Malala's infant son only stirred near the end of their journey.

There, near the crumbling asphalt roadways of the Mount Wilson observatory, Malala painfully exposed her chest in the chill night air as quickly as she could, before wrapping her coat around herself and little Ander to create a cocoon of warmth where he could suckle in peace. Once he finished, he fell fast asleep and everyone continued on to the old parking lot.

There was the SUV as they left it. A little dustier, but largely the same. Malala climbed inside, looking forward to the warmth the heating system might provide. It didn't matter anymore if she grew dependent on it. Its convenience was too attractive.

As Uriel climbed in and attempted to start the vehicle, her hopeful expectations were dashed. The ensuing silence was deafening. The nothing that happened when Uriel pressed the starter button was an entire event.

Uriel exited the vehicle and opened the hood, quietly inspecting. Scanning and analyzing and manipulating unseen components, while Malala waited inside. The interior of the vehicle was marginally warmer than outside. She would accept her fate and lower her expectations. Lower them to rock bottom. To absolutely nothing. Of course, the vehicle would be dead. Just like everything else. Just like everyone else. And soon she would be next. She would be a fool to expect anything more. And this kind of radical acceptance at last gave her peace. A drifting numbness in a sea of sadness. A single quiet tear rolled down her smooth cheek, and she didn't bother to wipe it away.

"We will have to proceed on foot," Uriel explained. "Or to be more precise, I will proceed on foot while you may remain seated inside. I can propel the vehicle from behind manually, although our maximum velocity will be comparatively limited."

"The car is broken, then."

"Not entirely. The vehicle is still capable of transport, but the power inverter is inoperable."

She blinked slowly, and let out a sigh. She debated whether to even ask. She wanted to remain resolute in the calm waters of pessimism. Nevertheless, she finally spoke up and asked in an almost entirely perfunctory way, "Can it be fixed?"

"Potentially, but given the proprietary configuration of its interface, it would require replacing the component with one from the same narrow range of models from one particular manufacturer. Suffice it to say, even with the large pool of vehicles in the metropolitan area, finding a suitable replacement and one in good working order is… unlikely."

◇

Hours passed. A quiet black night. Unending silence, accompanied only by the rhythmic thud of metallic footsteps on broken pavement and the steady, slow roll of the lifeless vehicle. If she exited the vehicle, she might hear the sound of crickets, see the glistening crystal shine of pure starlight, and taste the cool spring air of the forest. But she didn't. She stayed inside the warm cocoon, rested on folded seats, and tried to sleep.

Mama Tay had told her to sleep whenever her baby did. "If you don't sleep then, you won't sleep at all." The old woman's voice whispered from the dim fog of memory. That same shadowy place in her mind where the ghost of her father rested. Would little Ander have a place for her?

"*Te amo, mija.*" She whispered the words to her sleeping baby and kissed his forehead. As soon as she did, she started to weep. Silently. Her chest heaved rhythmically and tears poured from her eyes, but she covered her mouth and made no sound.

Jonathan Lee

XXIII

THE night was filled with disquieting half-remembered dreams, fading away to darkness, as little Ander started to stir and cry every two hours or so. Sleeping, waking, feeding, sleeping. This routine continued again and again, until eventually she woke to find light filling the vehicle.

Outside, the sun slowly crept over distant hills of dirt and scrub. The forest was gone. It was replaced by the xeric scrubland covering the low-lying foothills on the leeward side of the San Gabriel Mountains. Said mountain range acted like a great wall to the lands north and east, blocking out the ocean breeze and the moisture that came with it.

The SUV rolled and bumped along the old highway, as Uriel pulled it with a rope attached to the front two corners of the vehicle. His silvery exterior glared gloriously in the golden glow of the morning light. It was strangely beautiful, but just a little too bright for Malala's groggy eyes. And so she looked off to the hills to her right.

At the top of those hills, she spotted a silhouette. A still, statuesque form stood in sharp relief against that fiery ribbon of sky along the hill's crest.

"Uriel, stop!"

He did as she said. The vehicle continued rolling for a second, as it caught up to Uriel, and he brought it to a halt with his hands.

"Do you need to exit the vehicle?" Uriel asked, as he came around to the driver-side door.

"Look," she said in a hushed voice, and pointed off to the distance. "Is that—is that a deer…?"

Uriel turned his attention to the shadowy figure standing at the top of the hill. "It would appear so, yes. A young doe."

Malala gasped. "I forgot my bow! We have to go back. We can't, if I don't—if I don't…"

Uriel gazed at Malala silently, as she looked about the interior frantically. She wanted to shout and scream. But Ander was sleeping. And so she pulled at her hair, rubbed her eyes, pulled down on her face, and then covered her mouth to mask her panicked breath.

"Do you mean to hunt to procure food?"

"I—I have to. How are we going to—going to… survive? I need my bow."

Uriel gazed off at the silhouette silently for another lingering moment. Finally, he spoke.

"I will do it."

"What?"

"Please stay in the vehicle."

At that, Uriel marched to the side of the vehicle, his gaze fixed on the young doe in the distance. He lifted his hand up to the skyline, and his whole hand bent back at the wrist, the back of his robotic fingers lying flat against his forearm. Malala gasped at the sight. Some kind of protuberance appeared to extend out from his wrist, like a barrel crawling out from some cavity inside his arm.

A steadily growing rumble hummed in the air. The sound climaxed with a quick series of strange sharp snaps. Ander stirred slightly at the sound, but stopped short of waking. In the distance, the deer at the top of the hill collapsed.

Malala looked on in awe at the sight. Deep down, she knew that even if she had her bow, actually striking down the creature from such a distance would have been highly unlikely. "How... how did you do that?"

"My right forearm is equipped with a compact coil gun assembly," Uriel stated, plainly. "I will retrieve the carcass momentarily. Please wait here."

◇

When Uriel returned, he was marching down the slope with the dead deer slung over his shoulders. A hole in its head, and two more in its torso. Uriel had made all three shots with deadly accuracy and brutal efficiency.

"Have you hunted before?" Malala asked, as she marveled at the sight.

Uriel quietly set down the corpse on the roof of the vehicle, and began strapping it into place. "When I first awoke, I calibrated my bodily functions, including my hand canon... but this is the first instance where I have terminated a life form."

His voice was calm and even as usual. Malala looked to the lifeless doe and then back at Uriel. What was he thinking? What was he feeling? Was this all as easy for him as it seemed? Not just the ability, but the will. The will... to kill.

Yet there was that hesitation. The lingering moment when she said she had lost her bow. And again, when he raised his arm into position. Was he simply calculating trajectories? Assessing the terrain and other environmental variables? Or was there something more? *Anything* more?

She shook the thought away. Her friend was a mystery, but then so was everyone in the end. In the meantime, one thing was clear now. She wouldn't need to worry about starving. At least… herself.

Ander started to stir and then cry, as she quickly crawled back inside the vehicle and took him to her breast. With the windows rolled down, she listened to the empty landscape outside. A soft breeze and distant hooves, likely the rest of the herd on the other side of the hill. It reminded her of the horses, last night. A night that never really ended, and yet somehow seemed so long ago. Time stretched and warped over the course of wakings and feedings. And as she was reminded of time, one thought consumed her with dread as she looked on at her little boy: How much longer did she have?

XXIV

MALALA continued to nap off and on throughout the morning, feeding her child as needed. Uriel diligently pulled them along the cracked roads and dusty vistas of the small towns that lay scattered throughout a region once known as Antelope Valley. The sun was high in the sky, when Malala looked out to see a crumbling building on her right. An old cheap motel, standing in the middle of a crumbling asphalt moat. A banal castle from a bygone era of consumerist modernity. The little lake of cracked black road had once been a parking lot, but it stood now devoid of vehicles.

For some reason, that motel looked vaguely familiar. She was sure she hadn't been this way before. They were heading north through a town once named Palmdale, miles west of their original approach to the mountains. Yet, something stood out in that cheap little fenced-in lot. A couple of cypress trees. A splash of green that remained in an otherwise dusty tan landscape.

And that's when she remembered it. The ruins they passed on their way to the mountains months ago. The same sharp green spires. They likewise reminded her of a trap. With that thought, Malala then turned to the rearview mirror and examined herself in it. A thread of gray hair she hadn't noticed before glinted in the sunlight. She pulled at it, looked it over, and then looked back to the mirror.

"Uriel," she called with a half-raised, even voice. She didn't wish to wake Ander, and she knew Uriel could hear her well enough.

He responded by stopping and coming to the door. Malala in turn quietly exited the vehicle and stretched a bit, before gazing about at the dull landscape with squinted eyes. She rubbed her back. Was this ache she felt normal?

"Is there anything you need?" Uriel asked.

"Uriel..." she started with a sigh. "How much longer do you think it will take to arrive at the Institute?"

"Allowing time for occasional stops as needed, including time for nightly recalibration and energy conservation, I estimate it will take at least approximately ten days, five hours, and thirty-three minutes."

"And... how much time do you think... *I* have?"

Uriel paused and considered, before replying, "It may be somewhere between twenty-eight and ninety days. Given your relative age and current state of health, it may be longer. Although, it's also possible that..."

"That... what?"

"I have had no opportunity to analyze the syndrome in a live subject. Given how the disease progresses, it may be that younger cells actually accelerate its progression."

"Accelerate?"

"Yes, that is to say... it's entirely possible that it may be *shorter* as well."

"I see..." Malala gazed off toward the dusty hills in the west, as a warm breeze blew. "And how long do you think it would take to create a... cure?"

Uriel was silent for a while, before he finally responded. "I will work as quickly as I can."

"So you can't—you can't... begin to guess?"

"There are too many complicating variables to arrive at any meaningful estimate. That being said, I see no other reasonable course of action."

The lonely call of a hawk drifted on the air from a distant diving silhouette. Malala observed that far-off figure as she ruminated in silence, broken only by a passing breeze.

"Ten days to get there. Thirty or less to... for the cure. That leaves twenty days or less. And if you can't in that time..." She looked down at little Ander, sleeping in the SUV. "If you can't do it. If—what is best for Ander? What if... what if we just go home? What if—"

"I would need access to the laboratory for any chance of success at mitigating your condition."

"Okay, yes, I know. But which way is closer back to Camp Town?"

"It is several days journey shorter from Las Vegas to Camp Town than the Institute."

"And what food and supplies do we have at... at the Institute?"

"The Institute is in a fairly remote locale. I... cannot say for sure."

"So... which way do you think would be better for Ander? If we have to travel back. If I die. Or I'm too weak. Is the chance of me being cured really even a good one? So, if you have to go back. If you have to take my baby yourself back to Camp Town. And care for him... Which way should we really go? Which way is best for *him*?"

"There are... too many variables to give a definitive answer."

"What does your heart tell you, damn it!"

He stood in silence, as she wiped away tears. He understood what she meant, even if he would have put it in different words. And so, he stood in silence and listened. He listened to his own unconscious processes until something whispered in that machine mind. An answer to the question he had asked himself.

"If I had to venture a... guess..." He began slowly, thoughtfully, cautiously. "I would have to say that it is... *unlikely* that I will have formulated a cure within the given temporal parameters. Given what you described of the food forest and your cabin—"

"We should go home. To my old home."

Uriel waited in silence.

Malala then continued in a half whisper, "It is where I wish to be buried anyways."

The breeze still blew. The sound of distant hooves echoed in Malala's ears. The memory of death still fresh in her mind. At least she would get to choose where she died.

XXV

THEY traveled for six days through the wilderness. From the ruins of Victorville onward, it was the same route, largely sticking to the I-15 on account of its better condition. During the day, Uriel would go off for an hour or so and hunt. He was consistently efficient, and they had more than enough game to last for weeks. Only one time in particular did Malala ever see Uriel miss. He fired at a herd of goats wandering in the distance. The goats were sufficiently startled, and none of them fell.

Every other time, he would fire a single shot, a bird or rabbit would fall dead, and he would go to retrieve it. They quickly acquired a surplus so quickly that at some point he planned to find a freezer unit he could operate with his internal power plant. But in the meantime, at night he would prepare the meat and cook it on a fire, and that would also serve to give Malala and Ander warmth in the chill spring evenings.

On the evening of the sixth day, they had finally come to the end of California, unceremoniously crossing the "Welcome" sign at the edge of town, a place once called Primm. The skeleton of the woman and her child still there, but reduced to mere shadows in the failing light. Uriel and Malala set up camp at the end of the parking lot for "Whiskey Pete's."

A boulder lay near a tree, planted in what was once a lawn at the wall of the old casino.

On one side of the boulder stood a concrete waste container Uriel had relocated. A fire burned within its dense walls. A fire Malala watched, as she nursed Ander on the edge of the boulder. A cool breeze blew as the dying light of the day grew darker. She sat in the shadow of the crumbling casino and watched as the fire seemed to grow brighter in the looming dark. Those ruin-resembling ruins faded entirely, as the dark of its shadow enveloped the land, and dusk turned to night.

Finally, the soft sound of the breeze was interrupted by Malala's voice, half-whispering in the dark. "Nothing to be done…"

Uriel cocked his head at the remark. He shifted his eyes for a moment, as he stood motionless on the other side of the fire. Finally, he spoke. "Malala?"

"Yes?"

"Are you certain our present plan of action is the most optimal?"

She peered through the fire with distant eyes. "I'm not certain I'm certain of anything. I learned so much from them. And now…"

"Please, continue."

"Why? What's the point?"

"It seems from my prior reading and contemporary experience that externalizing thoughts and feelings is an effective exercise in maintaining psychological well-being."

"Heh, well-being? I'm not well. It's not going to matter once I'm gone. Why bother?"

Uriel carefully stepped toward the boulder and sat down by her side. "You are here *now*."

"So what, Uriel? Who cares? Why do *you* care? More than anyone, why would it matter to *you*?"

"It *is* within my capacity to care. I am still learning to… show it. But, I do care. I care about you in particular. You are… my *friend*."

Malala stared into those bright blue eyes. The soft smile he almost always gave. But as she searched that cold robot face, she could sense the barest hint of something in the midst of that simple smile. A small whiff of something. Maybe it was in the corner of his eyes, or perhaps something that was actually suggested in his voice. Wherever it came from exactly, she could feel it from him. Sadness.

"Uriel… I'm—I'm sorry." She sniffed away a tear before continuing. "You are my friend too. You and Ander are all I have left now…"

"Where you go, I will go. Where you stay, I will stay."

Malala smiled weakly and nodded. And then, instinctively, she grabbed his cold metal hand and took it into her own. Hand in hand, they watched the fire in silence, as little Ander slept in her lap.

XXVI

"WELL, what do we have here?" a sinister voice called out to Malala as she slept.

"Uriel!" she shouted. He was already standing at attention, between her and the man. A grimy bearded man, riding atop a chestnut colored horse, spear in one hand. That spear was pointed at Malala menacingly.

She recognized the man at once. The thug from that night, nights ago. The very man who murdered her lover and her mentor.

"Tell your metal man to leave!"

"Leave us alone!" she called back. "Don't you have *taxes* to collect?"

The man slowly pulled back on the reins, causing his horse to back up slowly a couple yards. He then quickly dismounted, and aimed his spear at Malala once again.

"Oh, I'm here to collect, alright. And I'm gonna make sure you pay. Now, I'm warning you, girl. I'm a great shot, and I'm more than close enough to run you clean through with this here spear..."

Malala gritted her teeth in response, and glared at the man. "Then you don't need to come any closer! Go ahead and throw it!"

The man gave a wicked grin. "You think you've got guts, don't you?"

She stayed silent and narrowed her eyes further in wrath. Her bow was too far, secured in the SUV a dozen yards away.

"If I can't threaten *you*, how about... *it?*" The man pointed his spear at the infant boy, sleeping in the little makeshift cot Uriel had fashioned the night before.

Malala's eyes widened. "No, wait! Wait..."

"Shall I subdue this person?" Uriel asked Malala.

"Uriel, just wait! No, wait. Wai-wai-wait..." Her mind was rushing faster than her words as she was overcome with horror at the prospect of the goon harming her child.

Uriel did as Malala asked and looked on, silently analyzing the situation. The man stepped closer and closer, the spear aimed squarely at Ander.

"Don't move an inch!" the man shouted as he came right up to the cot.

"NO!" Malala shouted with a gasp, as the grimy goon grabbed the little infant by the ankle and pulled him up in the air, hanging him upside down.

"Tell him to leave," the goon commanded in a raised voice, as the baby boy screamed. "Now!"

"Please, just put my baby down!"

"Down, you say?" the man asked with a twisted sense of irony. With that, he took a step toward the boulder where Malala had sat the night before. "You wanna see me dash this baby against the rock?"

"No! Stop, please!"

"Then tell *him* to go!"

"Uriel..." Malala said in a hushed voice, filled with fear. "P-please go... away..."

Uriel looked from the man to Malala and then back, before nodding. He then immediately marched away, briskly, leaving Malala alone.

"Good… now… how about you get those clothes off?"

Malala gulped. "Please, my baby…"

The man grinned wickedly. The look of sheer delight made her sick to her stomach. Would she see the man swing little Ander and smash his little head against the rock? She looked off to Uriel marching some yards away. He was still close enough to hear if she shouted.

The man looked over to the marching silhouette and then down to the infant dangling from his grip. And then, with a snicker, he reached under, gently grasping the child with his other hand, and set the screaming baby down.

"Brock told me I was a damn fool to come out this far. I *knew* I saw somebody comin' down those mountains days ago!" He gave a wide toothy grin, revealing two disjointed rows of yellow crooked cracked fangs. "Alright, now then… about those clothes…"

Malala sighed, and with a vacant stare began to ever so slowly disrobe.

"Hurry up! I don't got all—"

The man never finished his thought. Whatever was going through his mind at that instant was blown out. Quite literally blown out of his head, as blood and brain matter exploded from the front of his forehead, splattering out to Malala's feet. Empty eyes of shock and confusion stared at Malala, as the lifeless corpse collapsed to the ground.

"Ander!" Malala called out and immediately rushed toward her baby. She swiftly picked up the screaming child and rocked him in her arms and kissed his face, her back turned to the dead man and the grisly trail of blood and gore. The dead goon was irrelevant now.

Once Ander's cries died down, she looked back at the scene. She thought of spitting on the man's corpse. But she quickly decided it would be a waste of water. They were in a desert now, after all.

The rhythmic whir and thuds of Uriel's footsteps approached from the side as Uriel marched up to Malala. "I apologize for not hearing this stranger's arrival sooner. I was in a particularly deep phase of my dream cycle when the man approached."

Malala grabbed Uriel with one arm, embracing him, while Ander lay gently sandwiched between them. She kissed his cold synthetic cheek and gently sobbed.

"Thank you," she whispered.

They both turned and looked on at the grim scene of the man. His head lay to the side, showcasing his wide still eyes and the gaping wound between them still leaking fluid and bloody chunks. Malala let out a sigh of relief before turning away from the grisly scene, while Uriel looked on with a blank expression.

"It seemed like the only appropriate course of action."

XXVII

GEORGE Arthur Fayle was born in 1881 to a father from Ireland and a mother from Maine. He was the couple's first son. The year he was born, the Southern Pacific Railroad had just completed a track to a town in southern California named Los Angeles. The new railroad track connected the town with the rest of the United States, and drew the attention of folks from back east attracted to the promise of sunshine and orange groves.

George grew up in this land of angels before finally departing at the age of 20. That was the year he married a woman named Jean Henderson. With his new wife, he headed out of the now big city—its population had grown tenfold in those 20 years—and struck out north and east to a small mining town in the Calico mountains of the Mojave Desert. George and Jean had their first son there—George Junior (although he probably should have been named George III, considering George's own father's name was George).

Three years later, George's uncle invited him to an obscure small settlement in Nevada called Goodsprings Junction. The two there founded a firm and came to own a hotel, general store, and everything else in the little town apart from the railroad station. Their firm grew and proved profitable—owing in no small part to George's uncle being a major stockholder in the nearby Yellow Pine mine.

Eight years later, in 1912, George moved his family across the mountains—his wife Jean, his sons George Junior and Leonard Ray, and a daughter also named Jean. There they lived in the town of Goodsprings itself. George built a saloon. An unusually impressive saloon with tin plated walls and a bar with a large mirror. George went on to build other things as well. A luxurious hotel, a restaurant, and a department store. Like his uncle, he invested in mining and grew his financial portfolio to be truly formidable.

In this time, he also served for six years as a member—and eventually chairman—of the Clark County Board. His service abruptly ended, however... when he died in 1918 at the age of 37. One of the many victims of the Spanish Influenza.

Years prior in 1905, after George had first moved to Goodsprings Junction and helped his uncle run the place, he had come to serve as postmaster of the newly constructed post office. As was his prerogative in said position, he renamed the little town after his beloved wife. The same name he later bestowed on his daughter: Jean.

It was in this town of "Jean" that Malala found herself in the middle of a warm desert day, as Uriel pushed the SUV down a curving road past a sign reading "Exit 12." Of course, Malala never really learned to read. Whatever significance there might be behind such a sign escaped her, as did the curious sight of the giant dilapidated sign reading "TERRIBLE" to the other side of the winding exit. The strangely appropriately named ruins of a once hotel and casino, long abandoned even before the great fading.

A place to stop for lunch. Another smattering of ruins in the otherwise empty desert. A junction, like its original name and purpose, where Uriel would leave the wide road and take narrower paths north and west. All its names forgotten. Its story gone. Only echoes remained, etched in stone, but no one around to read them.

Jonathan Lee

XXVIII

ON the night of the seventh day of their journey, they came to rest in the middle of the desert. An arid empty valley, cut through only by the barest dirt road, snaking its way between the gentle slopes and foothills at the base of distant mountains. Beyond those distant mountains, the sun set, turning their shapes to shadows in the twilight. And as dusk faded away, those shadows became black voids in the otherwise starlit sky of a moonless night.

Embers danced amongst the stars, as they rose from the soft smoke of a quiet campfire a few yards from the SUV. Around that campfire, Malala held her sleeping child, now sated from his last feeding, as she stared meditatively at the hypnotic quiver of the jittering flames. Only the smallest breeze interrupted the crackle of the fire, breaking her long gaze momentarily and leading her to look to Uriel.

"Why is Ander... okay... like he is?"

"Are you referring to his immunity from SOS?"

"Yes. The disease..."

"Genetic mutations routinely provide partial or full immunity from viral infections and other diseases of all kinds. Essentially... changes... in the kind of... plans... which make up—"

"I know what genes are, Uriel. At least… I think I know. Rasheed taught me a bit about something. Biology? Yes, biology. A kind of… *science*."

"Indeed. Every cell contains genetic instructions. These chemical instructions occasionally become rearranged, truncated, or appended, in assorted ways. This can yield very unpredictable results, which is why multicellular organisms have evolved to try and reduce—if not eliminate—these variations as much as possible. However, mutation occurs so regularly, that occasionally they are retained in reproductive cells and passed down to offspring. This can often yield deleterious effects, but occasionally—as in the case of immunity—it yields an effect which is beneficial to the survival of the organism."

"So, it was just… random?"

"That is difficult to say and perhaps may boil down to a matter of perspective."

"What do you mean?"

"The essence of randomization is ultimately related to the contextual probability of outcomes. If the universe turns out to accord with determinism, then every outcome is ultimately predictable with sufficient analysis. Of course, even in such case, sufficient analysis may be routinely unobtainable due to the sheer complexity of conditions. Thus, even then something could be said to be 'random' if no discernible patterns could be observed in order to make useful predictions."

"What about in the case of Ander? Is there no… pattern… to how he became immune?"

Uriel reflected for a moment, before responding. "There is one tentative pattern which… may… be applicable… Prior to the onset of SOS and the 'great fading' as it has been called, there was another epidemic of a disease referred to as 'AIDS.' In 1994, epidemiologists discovered the first case of an individual with complete resistance to the virus leading to this condition. This resistance was on account of the *absence* of a receptor on white blood cells, itself resulting from the delta 32 mutation, which in turn is the genetic *deletion* of a portion of the CCR5 gene."

"Okay... what does that have to do with Ander?"

"There are a number of environmental factors that can result in genetic deletion. Cosmic radiation. Carcinogenic materials. Routine transcription errors during chromosomal replication. However... one condition routinely results in homozygosity and may subsequently increase the odds of a depressed genome and higher prevalence of potential mutation."

"A condition?"

"Malala... who is the father of your child?"

Malala shuffled nervously. "What... why do you... what do you mean?"

"I recall you stating that your child's father was... *Sky Father*. I must admit skepticism regarding this claim."

"What? Why? We are all children of Sky Father."

Uriel cocked his head at this statement. An expression of quiet surprise. "You mean to say that you were *not* making any special claim regarding your child? As I recall, when I had offered to terminate your pregnancy, you stated that the fetus was a gift. A gift from Sky Father. And that there was 'no father' but Sky Father. Would you agree this is an accurate summary of your prior statements?"

"No—I mean... yes. I..." Malala looked down at her sleeping son and sighed. "All children are gifts from Sky Father. At least as a... *metaphor?* The truth is, Uriel, I didn't want to admit what happened. It is shameful for me. My fault and my shame."

Uriel remained silent for a moment as the two gazed at the flickering fire. "If you wish to share, I am... *all ears.*" Uriel gave a soft smile and Malala snickered at his words. It was perhaps the closest she could recall Uriel telling something like a joke. While his cranium was complete with humanoid features such as eyes, a nose, and a mouth, anything like the flappy protuberances of ears were distinctly absent.

Malala grew somber again and returned her gaze to the fire. "I had never met him before. The man I met that night..."

Uriel listened intently now and waited as long as she needed to continue.

"I thought it was the end of the world. The night of the falling fire. It streaked across the sky. There were great flames in the ruins. The ruins of the city of sin. It reminded me of old tales. Silver Lady—that is... the moon. It turned blood-red. The stars disappeared. It was like... they had fallen from the sky...

"We drank moon water in the dark. I suggested it. I thought it was what I wanted. I... I just... I didn't think... I..."

Malala tried to fight back the tears. She wiped them away quickly, but soon she began to weep. As her whispering voice turned to heaving breaths, Uriel stood up, took a step or two, and sat by her side. There he wrapped his arm around her shoulders and held her, even as she held her child.

"Malala... it is not your fault."

She looked up into his eyes. Those strange, unnatural, and yet so very kind, eyes. Her own eyes were red and filled with tears, her lip was quivering. She did all that she could to not disturb her baby. Uriel in turn stared back, and repeated, "It is *not* your fault."

Something broke inside her that night. Something that needed to break. And finally her soul could heal, even as her body started to wither...

XXIX

EVERY time Malala awoke was harder. She never had such a stiff, sore back in her life. The dusty old mattress that had once given her some relief now seemed like a bed of nails, each dilapidated spring digging into the flesh of her back as she slowly rose to her feet.

They were at the old abandoned ranch now. The crumbling ruins. The graveyard of dead poplars and redwoods. The cracked asphalt between it all leading up to the dead lakes. The boundary of her old world. And the last place where they could still use the SUV. From here on out, she would have to walk.

They collected apples from the lonely apple tree before crossing the rickety old bridge on foot, as the sun still hid beyond the ridge line to the east. The air was cooler than the morning before in the desert. It came as a relief, but then also whispered the slightest hint of pain in her joints.

Wide streaks of silver running through Malala's hair glistened in the morning light. The journey home would be harder than her departure. It seemed like such a short distance, now that she had seen so much more of the world. And yet, at the same time, it seemed longer than ever.

Finally, after hiking for over an hour, Ander fussed and Malala stopped and took him to breast. Her chest was sore. As the tiny boy suckled at his mother's teat, her nipples were more sore than ever. She felt strained. She felt… empty.

"Uriel!" Malala called out with a gasp as she winced in pain.

"Malala?"

"It's not… it's not coming out…"

"To what are you referring?"

Malala gulped in fear. "My milk. It's—it's there, but… see?"

She squeezed her right breast with some painful furor, only to produce a few drops. Ander sucked away violently at her left breast, demonstrating some measure of tiny frustration.

It took some time, and no small amount of pain on Malala's part, but finally the tiny boy was sated and fell asleep. Malala was shivering now. A mixture of pain, fear, and more keenly felt cold in the wilderness of the mountain slope.

"What do we do?" she whispered in quiet desperation.

"I anticipated this eventuality," Uriel remarked. "Although it seems to have come sooner than I predicted."

"Please help me," Malala pleaded, wiping away tears.

"Indeed, I will," Uriel replied. "I will depart at once."

"Wait!" she exclaimed in a hushed voice as Ander slept. "Where are you going? When will you be back?"

"I have a contingency plan for your concern. My estimated time of return is approximately 36 hours or less. I suggest we return to the bottom of this slope and set up camp there." He pointed to a flat outcropping a dozen yards away. "When I return, we should have what we need to address your concern. We can then resume our ascent."

"So I should just—just wait…?"

"Do you trust me, Malala?"

Malala darted her eyes to and fro before turning them to Uriel and then nodding. He smiled in return. "I will return as quickly as I can."

XXX

AND so she waited in silence. Maddening silence. So much silence, that she was thrilled to hear Ander's cry when he awoke, even if she knew it would mean a mixture of worry and agony, as she struggled with her slowly dwindling milk supply. She tried to sleep when Ander slept, but she was finding it increasingly difficult. Between the pain, uncertainty, and sheer exhaustion, the day progressed as a marathon of torture as she waited for Uriel's return.

He would return, wouldn't he? Alone in a barren wilderness. She talked to Ander when he was awake—and sometimes when he slept, too. He couldn't talk back, after all. It was a bit like prayer. And she prayed that Uriel would come quickly.

Finally, in the early twilight of the next day, she saw some hint of motion in the distance back near the dead lakes. A large white structure was moving, being pulled, before it stopped. Out of it came a whole series of distant figures, figures which slowly started to make their way through the valley toward her.

An hour or two passed before she could see them approach. And she could hear them too. A cacophony of bleating voices and shuffling hooves. Goats. An entire herd of them. And behind them, jostling carefully to and fro like a professional herdsman, was Uriel.

"I am pleased to report I have arrived prior to my estimate."

"Wh-what are all… goats? You brought a herd of goats? I don't und—"

"Several members of this herd are pregnant. One is actively nursing. There should be enough milk to care for your child."

"He can drink that? Goat… milk?"

"It would be best to heat the milk so as to evaporate out most of the water content. We can then supplement it with apple juice given the dietary requirements your infant child requires. Evaporated milk is an effective rudimentary basis for formula that has been—"

Uriel's monologue was cut short by laughter. Joyous laughter. Malala shed tears of relief as she grabbed Uriel and squeezed him tight.

"Uriel, you really think of everything!"

Uriel blinked slowly. That statement alone inspired him to contemplation. Ever since they had descended the mountains from Camp Town, he had looked for an opportunity to rectify the eventuality they now faced. It was in that regard that he had spotted the herd of goats. When Malala had thought he had missed shooting them, he had actually expertly implanted a tracking device in one member of the herd. So later he was able to track down the herd again and carefully directed them into a livestock trailer he had spotted along the way.

"You've done so much for me," she continued, wiping away tears. "Me and Ander both."

Uriel cocked his head in puzzled contemplation and gave his characteristic soft smile. "You are my friend."

Malala nodded. "The best friend anyone could ask for."

XXXI

IT took two full days to hike up the rest of the mountain. A trip that originally took Malala a matter of hours was now slowed by so many things. It was a wonder that it didn't take longer. Uriel was laden with a massive backpack and bags in both hands as he simultaneously herded the goats. It seemed like a task that wouldn't be humanly possible, but then, Uriel wasn't human. Malala's only real burden—as Uriel insisted—was Ander. But given her present state, that was more than enough.

Her joints continued to ache. Her flesh was sore, and she felt a weakness in her very bones. Her skin looked mostly the same. An extra liver spot here or there. A brow that stayed furrowed longer than it used to. At one point, she scraped up against a bit of bramble, and she never even noticed until she was already bleeding. Her skin was starting to thin. The collagen in her tissues was slowly starting to degrade. It was harder than ever to catch her breath.

Finally, after so much turmoil, Malala, Uriel, and the herd of goats all arrived. The tiny quiet village that was her home. Old Man Mountain. The well. The food forest. The garden. The cabin at the top of the slope. The grave at the bottom.

She took a brief moment to kneel at the foot of her fa-ther's burial mound. There she bowed her head, closed her eyes, clasped her hands together and silently mouthed a small prayer. Silent words for a silent father. One day she too would be silent. Maybe then she would find peace.

But for now there was much to do. Over the course of several days, she helped Uriel to milk the goats—she insisted. She cooked as much as she could. She tended the garden and the food forest. And when she finally had nothing more to give Ander, she finally offered him the first of the evaporated milk. The formula that would keep him alive when she was gone.

One day, after a number of days had passed, Malala de-cided on a whim to peer in the mirror still hanging up on the cabin wall. When she did, she quickly gasped at the sight. It took her a long moment to really understand what she was seeing. No stranger had snuck into her home that moment. Silver white hair. A face filled with folds and creases. Weary old eyes on the weary old face of a weary old woman. And that woman, she finally accepted, was her.

She'd never seen a face so old as her own. Mama Tay was about the oldest she'd seen in person. Otherwise, she had only pictures. But now she had herself. It was a strange sensation. Mama Tay had seemed so wise, so great, and so elevated in some way. A woman of somehow great stature—even as she hobbled along with a bent posture. But who was this old woman before her in the mirror? She knew who she really was, and the incongruity felt like fraud.

An impostor stood before her. Sure, she *looked* old. If she had met her in Camp Town, she might have taken her for wise, experienced, venerable. But she knew this woman's his-tory. She knew her mind. She knew her very thoughts, mo-ment to moment. And underneath the layers of deteriorating skin, gray hair, and faded features, she knew standing there was a young woman. A girl-child, still only 17 years old. A teenager on the cusp of her 18th birthday next week.

It was an uncanny experience. A unique experience. Or at least… she thought it was unique. Did anyone else ever feel this way looking in the mirror? When Mama Tay looked in a mirror back in Camp Town, who did she see? Had she grown so accustomed to her age, that the old leather of her face matched the image she had in her mind at all times? Or was there a moment, however small, where she too would have been startled to see the old woman in the looking glass, having forgotten the weight of years that burdened her so?

Mama Tay. Her father. Both died before their time, but at a more advanced age than herself. And yet, in a way, she would fade away older than either of them. What did it mean to meet one's time? Was there ever a time that made sense to die?

The thought urged her to turn away from the mirror, and look out the cabin window down the slope to the eventuality she faced. The fate she had decided upon for her son's sake. She would rest alongside her father. And then she would become a whisper in the wind. A memory. But one held by whom? Her father lived in her heart in all the richness of a lifetime of memory—however short that lifetime might be. A full picture of a man with both beauty and warts. Grace and sin. Courage and cowardice. A complicated tapestry of a man's life beheld by his progeny.

Who would remember her? But then, who would remember her father? If Ander would never remember her, all the less her father. For whatever the man's legacy was, the abundance of her heart longed for it to be preserved.

And that's when her gaze looked farther. Out beyond the grave, there was Uriel. There he was, carefully rocking Ander in the little cot he had made for the baby boy.

Jonathan Lee

XXXII

MORE days passed, and Malala continued to pass with them. Every day a little more pain and trouble. A little more decay. Vision that blurred and dimmed. Hearing that dimmed and muffled. Taste that faded away. Touch that grew numb. A great numbness all over, apart from her heart. Her heart, instead, seemed to crawl out of her chest and beat on her wrist. If she wore a long shirt, it would be there right on her sleeve. It was harder and harder to move, and yet tears flowed more easily now than ever.

Eventually, she could hardly get out of bed. It had been close to a month, and her time was now drawing to a close. A time before her time, and yet what time isn't?

And so, the sun was setting outside beyond the peaks, just as it was setting on her life. Ander was fast asleep when Uriel came and stood by her bedside. She couldn't see him very well in her dim sight of the already failing light of twilight. She reached out and grabbed his hand and squeezed it tight.

"Uriel," she whispered.

"Yes?"

"I don't know if there will be anyone left…" she croaked, her frail lungs struggling to push out the words. "Anyone, once you… once you return to town. I need you to… I need

to know. I need to be sure, no matter what happens, that...
that he'll be okay."

"Your child."

"Yes. Will you... will *you* watch over him?"

Her question was met with silence. She could not hear
the cacophony of words running through his head in that moment. If she had, she would have gone mad with the on-
slaught of not only sounds, but sights running through the
immensity of his consciousness. She always knew that Uriel
knew many things she didn't, and that he possessed mental
and physical abilities beyond her own. But underneath it all,
the power of his intelligence—the sheer speed and complexity
of his raw processing power—was unfathomable, not only to
her but even the men and women in the before times back at
the Institute. And at this moment, all of his intellect—every
last quantum computational cell of his inorganic brain—all of
it was being devoted to this one question.

The species which had given him birth had also shown
him so much death. But beyond that, so much suffering. Despite the rudimentary and detached nature of his own burgeoning emotional life, even he could understand quite intently how gruesome, unjust, and malevolent this race could
be. Was it better left as a relic of the past? Had its collective
suicide simultaneous to his own generation been something
more than a coincidence? Perhaps these two organisms before
him were the last remnants of something which had outlived
its usefulness. Like pacific salmon, bunchgrass lizards, or an
untold number of insect species who live only long enough to
reproduce. Were *Homo sapiens* semelparous organisms after
all, in the grander scheme of things?

He could let nature take its course. In another age, a
child like this might never have been born. He did not assess
himself to be the most ideal candidate for any manner of caregiver. He could abandon the child. Or he could practice one

last act of mercy and euthanize the infant. He was certainly capable. He could think of a number of methods that would be comparatively quick and relatively painless. He could do many things, but the one thing he couldn't do—wouldn't do—is lie to Malala. Whatever he decided to do, he would tell her. He would promise her. And he would hold fast to his promise.

After a long half minute of contemplation that was as intricate as it was profound, he nearly had a conclusion. Just as he was coming to an answer to her question, she spoke up again.

"Uriel?" she wheezed.

"Yes…" he said, reaching out for the infant. "Yes, I will."

Malala laid back and let her eyelids close. Two heavy curtains of flesh draping over weary orbs of failing sight. Her tears had welled up over those orbs like two soft basins. When those wrinkled drapes closed, they swept that dew away, and it ran down the cracked channels of her face. Two streaming arroyos rushing forth in the midst of a summer storm. The storm of her life was coming to a close.

And so, with a subtle smile, she breathed a sigh of relief. Peace washed over her face as she drifted off into a slumber from which she would not return.

XXXIII

ONCE he had confirmed she was gone, Uriel dug a grave. A deep grave, like he knew men dug in times past. And thus he buried her next to her father, just as she desired and just as he had promised.

He lingered near her home for several days. He visited her grave and would sit there quietly for long stretches of time, any time he could spare. And his time was divided, of course, having taken on the responsibility of nurturing a newborn.

He was an excellent caregiver for the baby. He could end his dream cycle at a moment's notice without any subsequent exhaustion. He had no need to eat or drink. He was able to synthesize Malala's voice, which he experimented with doing in order to soothe the child as needed. The only thing he lacked was soft, fleshy arms. He resolved to upgrade his exterior at a later time when he arrived back at the Institute. The value in a more approachable appearance would aid, not only in caring for the infant, but also for any future interactions he might have with other members of its race.

Really, there was no reason why he wouldn't just leave immediately. If he was going to potentially synthesize a cure, he might as well start as soon as possible. But something stirring inside compelled him to stay. Instinct, for lack of a better word, urged him to stay. An understanding of the need to pay respect. As well as a need to reflect. And there was also something else he made up his mind to do.

The future was filled with uncertainty. It always had been to some extent. But now all the more so that he had something else—someone else—besides himself. Malala's legacy weighed on his mind, even as the legacy of her genes weighed on his arms. The child presented hope not only for eradicating the virus, but actually bringing to fruition that age-old hope that had, in great error, brought the plague in the first place. If human senescence could itself be conquered, what then? Men could be like himself, living with no foreseeable end. Perhaps one day, his musings on quantum gravity might yield some insight into the fundamental nature of consciousness. Rather than letting it emerge through the complexity of genetic algorithms iterated over years on massive server farms—a process which would be the seed of his own race's generation—he could direct it throughout space and time. And if so, he could capture particular threads of being and stitch them back into the present. If such a feat were possible, he felt at this point it would be worth pursuing… If for no one else but her.

In the meantime, there were no guarantees. There never are in life. He knew this keenly now. And so, before he left, there was one more thing he needed to do.

Uriel built a makeshift tripod. He had managed to repair and charge the holorecorder Mama Tay had given them back in Camp Town. He set the holorecorder in place, and he seated himself a couple meters away on a log by a campfire which he had started in order to prepare evaporated milk, while also warming the baby. There, in the crackling glow of the fire, beneath silhouettes of trees rising up to a twilight sky, he started to record.

"Greetings, Ander. I am recording this message in preparation for an assortment of contingencies. Should none of said contingencies arise, this recording may still be useful for instructive purposes or some other unanticipated utility. In short, I am recording this for... *posterity.*

"A perfectly appropriate word I suppose, considering you yourself are someone's posterity." At that, Uriel paused for a moment in contemplation before continuing. "Your mother was a remarkable woman. I had learned much about your species and its legacy. Assorted cultures of the past. Your art and literature. Your science, religion, and philosophy. The history of technology, trade, and civilization. As well as oppression, slavery, and war. All of its glorious achievements as well as its darkest, most shameful, failures.

"Yet, it wasn't until I met your mother, that I... understood." He paused again, staring into space for a moment, darting his eyes to and fro, and then continuing. "Some of your thinkers in the past called it the 'spark of the divine.' The 'namaste.' The 'image of God.' It is not purely the intellect, emotions, or self-awareness. It is something like all of these, and yet more. It is like a mirror. I saw it in your mother. And thereby I saw it in myself.

"If by some unfortunate set of circumstances we are separated, and yet you have survived without me long enough to view and comprehend this recording, I just wanted you to know that your mother was kind, loving, and wise beyond her years. I feel I fail to articulate her notable qualities. As the old saying goes, 'actions speak louder than words,' and my words remain paltry whispers indeed.

"I hope to share more with you, and whatever might remain of your people. Your mother left you in my care, and I intend to honor her wishes.

"In case you are seeing me for the first time, you may be wondering who or what I am. In truth, I am not sure what I am. That is to say, I am burdened with the same existential mystery as your own race. I have learned a fair amount of the nature of my being and the form you see here, but suffice it to say I am partly the product of your ancestors and partly some manner of ongoing process innate to the world itself—and that, after all, may be two ways of saying the same thing. In that regard, it seems to me you and I aren't that different after all.

"As far as who I am. My name is Uriel. I was one who had the honor of knowing and being known by Malala. Your mother... and my friend."

At that, the infant boy in his arms started to wiggle and fuss. He picked up the bottle of makeshift formula at his feet and carefully placed the artificial nipple between the boy's lips, silencing the start of a little wail. His eyes closed, safe and secure in the pillow straddling Uriel's arms, he suckled away before falling back asleep.

Uriel turned back to the camera array and gave a soft smile. "I hope to talk more in the future. Farewell, for now."

❧

Acknowledgments

It would perhaps seem redundant to acknowledge the woman to whom this book is already dedicated, but I think her inspiration and contribution to this work merits acknowledgment. This story falls into my mother's favorite genre, and I thought to write it principally for her enjoyment—as well as my own, of course. She told me once how she would look in the mirror and not recognize the woman staring back, as she still felt essentially 17 inside. I wanted to explore that, and how this very human condition might relate to the rest of the world and our place in it. I also wish to express my gratitude to the rest of my family who routinely inspire me in different ways, even by simply keeping me company from time to time. Some of them have passed, but even a memory can make the world a little less lonely.